Xmas in the Arms of an ATL Shooter

Ca$h & Destiny Skai

Lock Down Publications and Ca$h Presents

Xmas in the Arms of an ATL Shooter

A Novel by *Ca$h & Destiny Skai*

Ca$h & Destiny Skai

Lock Down Publications
P.O. Box 944
Stockbridge, Ga 30281

Visit our website @
www.lockdownpublications.com

Lock Down Publications
Like our page on Facebook: Lock Down Publications @
www.facebook.com/lockdownpublications.ldp

Book interior design by: **Shawn Walker**
Edited by: **Shawn Walker**

Stay Connected with Us!

Text **LOCKDOWN** to 22828 to stay up-to-date with new releases, sneak peaks, contests and more…

Thank you!

Submission Guideline

Submit the first three chapters of your completed manuscript to ldpsubmissions@gmail.com, subject line: Your book's title. The manuscript must be in a .doc file and sent as an attachment. Document should be in Times New Roman, double spaced and in size 12 font. Also, provide your synopsis and full contact information. If sending multiple submissions, they must each be in a separate email.

Have a story but no way to send it electronically? You can still submit to LDP/Ca$h Presents. Send in the first three chapters, written or typed, of your completed manuscript to:

LDP: Submissions Dept
Po Box 944
Stockbridge, Ga 30281

DO NOT send original manuscript. Must be a duplicate.

Provide your synopsis and a cover letter containing your full contact information.

Thanks for considering LDP and Ca$h Presents.

Dedications

I would like to dedicate this book to all my loyal readers who have waited almost 5 years for me to release something new. No excuses but my publisher duties haven't allowed me time to write lately. Lock Down Publications has grown tremendously over the years. As you know, 85% of our authors are incarcerated. I've been dedicated to helping those brothers and sisters get their work published. However, after writing this book with my co-author, Destiny Skai, I believe my creative juices are flowing again.

Also, be on the lookout for my first movie. TIL MY CASKET DROPS, coming this summer. Before I let y'all begin reading XMAS IN THE ARMS OF AN ATL SHOOTER, I want to thank each and every one of you for always supporting me. Love y'all.

Last but not least, after serving 27 years in prison, I was paroled in September of 2018. The day I walked out of those gates I left many good men behind. I just want to say that I'll always do my best to represent y'all souljahs well. And if the parole board look at what I've done since I was granted clemency on a Life plus 30 years sentence, they'll know that many of you are deserving of the same second chance I was granted.

Much love,
CA$H

Chapter One

The loud sound of the job phone was driving Aria crazy. It had been ringing non-stop since she punched in at eight o'clock that morning. That was two hours ago. Wednesdays were always hectic, but what made it more painful was the fact that she had to be in the office that day. Once the COVID-19 pandemic hit, the office closed down and the employees worked from home with the exception of coming in once a week. However, Aria preferred to stay home so she could lounge, process claims, and answer the phone in her pajamas.

After graduating from a local community college, Aria landed a job with the insurance company, Progressive, as a claims adjustor. That wasn't her preferred profession, but it was in high demand and paid well. It allowed her to purchase and three-bedroom home and drive a Mercedes Benz GLE 53 AMG series, which meant there was no reason to complain.

"Good morning, Ms. Aria." The sound of Aria's supervisor, Pam, pulled her from the woods of Lala land and back into the busy office.

"Good morning, Pam," she replied dryly.

"I see that someone isn't in the Christmas spirit." Pam placed a card with a candy cane attached to it on her desk, along with a gift bag.

"Aren't you festive today?" Pam was wearing a Santa hat and an ugly sweater with bells for the holiday contest.

"I am, but I see that you're not."

"Nope! I just want to get my hours and go home. I participated in the gift exchange. That's all I can do."

"You didn't get laid last night and it shows," Pam stated as she adjusted her sweater. "Stop being a Grinch. It is the season to be jolly. So, when you leave here, go straight to the liquor store and jingle bell on that man's balls when you get home. I guarantee you'll feel better."

"Bye, Pam. I have work to do and so do you."

"Touché." Pam winked and walked away.

Aria had no rebuttal in place because Pam was right. She didn't have sex last night, which was partially the reason for her sour mood. Aria's boyfriend of two years, Jaheim, didn't get home until she was leaving out for work that morning and that alone infuriated her.

Jaheim was a dopeboy, but he wasn't pushing weight heavy enough for him to be out at all hours of the night. But for the past two months, it had been routine for him to come home late, if at all, and missing in action the majority of the day. Aria had a feeling he was cheating, but couldn't prove it. Whenever she checked his phone, there was never anything incriminating that could prove what she felt in her heart. So, in the meantime, she'd let it go. But on her way to work, Aria prayed that God gave her a sign to ease the confusion in her mind.

With the phones steadily ringing and emails coming in back to back, the hours flew by fast and before Aria knew it, it was time for her lunch break.

"Thank God," she sighed after staring at the clock and logging off of her computer.

Aria grabbed her purse from the desk and made a beeline outside to her SUV. Unlocking the door, Aria climbed inside and blasted the AC. The Florida sun was beaming despite the fact that it was winter, so it didn't take much for her to bust a sweat as she walked through the parking lot.

Aria took her phone out of her purse and unlocked the screen. She noticed there wasn't a single call from Jaheim or a text message, but a few were sitting in her DM on Instagram.

Aria smiled and shook her head when she saw that one of the messages was from a rapper named Young Milli from Atlanta. "This boy won't take no for answer." Granted she wasn't interested in anything beyond a friendship, Ari had to admit that it felt good to have a man of his status applying pressure to meet up on a more personal level. They had been following each other for a while and always commented and left hearts on one another's pictures. Young Milli was fine in Aria's eyes, but she couldn't see herself involved with a man in the rap industry.

Ari's smile quickly faded and her heart rate increased rapidly when she opened up the message from a chick named *JahJahs_Mommy*. The iPhone eleven clutched in her hand vibrated violently as she scrolled through photos of Jaheim lying in bed with a woman and a baby on his chest. If there was any uncertainty on what she was looking at, the message cleared that up immediately.

The message read: *I'm coming to you as a woman since Jaheim hasn't told you what's going on between us. Two months ago, I had his baby and when he's not home with you, he's here with me and our baby. He kept saying that he was going to tell you, but it's obvious that he didn't. I sent the pictures so that you can see it for yourself.*

Heavy tears coated Ari's eyelids and slid down her smooth, brown cheeks. Her heart that was tainted was now fully broken into a million, tiny pieces. Filled with rage and pain, she scrolled down to his name and pressed send. The phone rang several times before he picked up.

"What's up, babe?"

"You have a baby and didn't fucking tell me?"

"What?" There was slight hesitation in Jaheim's voice.

"Nigga, don't play stupid. You know what the fuck I'm talking about. I saw the pictures."

"What pictures?"

"The bitch sent me pictures of y'all on IG and told me everything. Bruh, you are so fucking foul for that. I swear. I knew I should've left you when you cheated with her the first time. But, nah, my dumbass took you back." Aria sniffled as she expressed the deepest pain she'd felt in a long time.

Jaheim took a deep breath and ran his hand across his face. That wasn't the way he wanted her to find out about his son. The second she brought it up Jaheim knew that Mya was behind it. For months, he'd managed to keep his secret buried. He knew that Aria was going through his phone, so he purposely left it out and unlocked. But, the incriminating phone he used to communicate with Mya was left inside his car at all times.

"Babe, I'm sorry. I swear I was going to tell you. I just didn't know how or the right time to tell you."

"There is no right time to confess that you been cheating and got another bitch pregnant." Ari put the phone on speaker and set it on her thigh. Squeezing the steering wheel, she let out a huge wail from deep within her diaphragm. This situation was the straw that broke the camel's back.

"You right and I'm sorry. I didn't mean to hurt you. I swear I didn't. That was the last thing I wanted to do." His confession was spoken just like a serial cheater. "I'ma kill this bitch!"

"Why? Because she told me the truth when you couldn't?" Aria wiped the tears from her eyes and leaned her head against the steering wheel. "Jaheim, it's over. I can't do this with you anymore. I will pack up your shit and sit it on the porch."

"Come on, Aria, don't do this. We can talk about this later when you get home."

"I'm good. It's over. You can pick up your shit and take it to Mya's house since that's where you been staying when you wasn't coming home." Aria laughed. Not because it was funny, but out of hurt. "At least I know why you haven't been home."

"Aria, baby, please."

"I swear I'm good this time. Bye!"

Aria ended the call and went back inside of the office to find her supervisor. Pam was on the phone when Aria walked into her office, but when she saw her co-worker's tear-stained face, she hung up abruptly. "Aria, is everything okay?"

"No. I need to go home."

"Do you want to talk about it?" Pam spoke with genuine concern in her voice. She was like the office mom and gave the best advice when it came down to real-life situations. Everyone needed someone like Pam in their corner.

"No."

"Okay. I won't pressure you." Pam walked up and wrapped her arms around Aria, locking her into a bear hug. "If you need me, please don't hesitate to call."

"I won't. Thanks, Pam."

"You're welcome." Pam released Aria from her warm embrace and lifted her chin. "Pray about it. I know your vacation starts next Friday and I won't see you until the New Year since we don't have to come in next week. Use that time to clear your head and remember that God will never put more on you than you can bear."

"Okay."

"Everything will work itself out," Pam promised.

"I hope so."

Aria left out of the office knowing the situation could never work out. Jaheim broke her down for the last time and there was no turning back no matter how many apologies, or gifts he showered her with. Their relationship had flat-lined for good. She called her best friend of twenty years, Brandy, so she could meet her at the house. Moral support was what she needed.

Aria and Brandy were more like sisters and she was the one person that she could confide in with no judgment.

When Aria pulled up into her driveway, Brandy was leaning against her car dressed in activewear and a fitted cap. She had changed into fight gear the moment Ari called her crying. Her hand gripped a baseball bat. The sight alone made Aria laugh as she climbed out of the SUV. "Brandy, why are you dressed like that and why do you have a bat?"

"In case we have to beat Jaheim's ass. You know he ain't gone leave just because you told him to. We gone have to make his ass crawl out of here."

"You are crazy!"

"I know." Brandy twirled the bat in her right hand. Back in high school, she was on the rifle team, so twirling weapons was her specialty. "Now, let's go in here and pack this nigga shit up. I hope you have some wine or liquor in here because we're going to need that."

"The bar is fully stocked, honey," Aria replied.

The girls were one hour into packing when the sound of *Pick Up Your Feelings* by Jazmine Sullivan blared through the soundbar on the entertainment system. Brandy sang for the love of the song. Aria sang because she felt the same pain.

Boy, please, I don't need you. Oh, oh, memories, all that shit, you can keep it. Don't forget to come and pick up your, oh, feelings.

Don't leave no pieces. Put a lock on the door where my heart once was, hmm. Boy, you had your fun. But I had enough. Now I'm really done. I deserve so much more than

*you gave to me. So now I'm saving me. And I made my peace.
So you can run them streets.*

Suddenly, the song cut off without warning and not a single sound could be heard. "Don't tell me your phone just died."

"It shouldn't be." Aria stopped throwing Jaheim's shoes in a bag so she could check her phone. "You know we have to back that…" Aria froze when she saw Jaheim enter the bedroom. "What are you doing here?"

Brandy took one look at Jaheim and turned to face him with her arms folded across her chest. She was ready to spray him in the face with the mace she had in her pocket and put her Louisville Slugger to work.

Jaheim caught the ill vibe from Aria's best friend. "Hey, Brandy."

"Jaheim."

"What are you doing here?" Aria asked again.

"We need to talk."

"I'm done talking to you." Aria stood back on her legs with her arms behind her back.

"Come on, Aria. You just gone throw away two years just like that? I made a mistake," he pleaded.

"Jaheim, you've been making a lot of the same mistakes over the years and I'm sick of it. There's nothing that you can say or do that will change my mind."

Jaheim moved closer to Aria and the whiff of marijuana graced her nostrils. "Let me make it up to you. I love you, Aria. I don't want to be with that girl."

Aria cocked her head to the side with knitted brows. "That's funny because y'all look like a happy family in those photos."

"I was only there to see my son. She took those pictures on her own. That girl knows that I don't want her. And she knows I'm not leaving you for her and now she's mad." Jaheim continued to plead his case.

"Boy, bye. Don't nobody wanna hear that bullshit. Just get your shit and move the fuck around because you blocking her view of a real nigga."

Jaheim cut his venomous eyes in the direction of Brandy. If looks could kill she would be on the floor. "Why don't you just mind your business, damn! I'm not talking to you. I don't even know why you are here."

"She is my business and I'm here to make sure," Brandy pointed her finger in his direction, "you don't try to slither your way back into her good graces, ole snake ass nigga. You should've been had your walking papers. And since you have so much to say, where the fuck were you when she had a miscarriage two months ago?"

To hear Brandy mention the miscarriage brought tears to Aria's eyes. Jaheim attempted to comfort Aria, but she pushed him away with great force. "Don't touch me," she screamed. "Just get your shit and get the fuck out now!"

"Are you happy now?" Jaheim's eyes were back on Brandy.

"Surely is. Bye!"

Jaheim didn't utter another word. He simply grabbed two of his bags and walked out of the room. After four trips he was gone. Aria and Brandy sat down on the sofa in the living room and sipped on some Casamigos with pineapple juice when a notification went off on Aria's phone.

"That better not be stupid texting you," she snarled with her face balled up.

"No. It's Instagram."

"It better not be that bitch or we going to beat her ass and that's on periodt!"

Aria unlocked the screen on her phone and smiled. "It's not her. It's that rapper, Milli."

"You mean as in fine Young Milli from Atlanta?"

"That's him."

"Hmm. Let me find out." Brandy was happy that it wasn't any drama coming her girl's way because she was ready to pull up. She wanted all the smoke when it came to Aria.

"Find out what? It's nothing. He likes me, but I'm not about to talk to him. This man is too popular and too fine. I know he has a busload of hoes waiting for their turn to be with him. I'm good on that. I left him on read, so now he's asking why am I ignoring his messages."

"Let me see." Aria passed her the phone. Brandy scrolled the chain of messages. "This man is trying to take you out and you was curving him for raggedy-ass Jaheim? You going on this date because I'm about to respond."

"No! Brandy don't do that. I just got out of a relationship. It's going to take me a minute to get over him. We were together for two years."

Brandy kept messaging Milli as she spoke. "You know what my mama told me? The way you get over one man is to get up under another one. So, do what you feel is best for you in that area. I can't tell you who to give your coochie to, but you are going on this date. End of story."

Another notification came through. "What is he saying?" Aria asked nervously. She knew that there was no telling what Brandy was saying to him.

"Ouuu, bitch. He wants you to come to Atlanta and spend Christmas with him."

"No, ma'am. I don't know him like that. He might kidnap me or some weird shit."

"Girl, please. This man ain't hardly pressed for coochie. He can hit up any one of these thirst buckets on his posts and fly them out and they will go. But, he wants you and I accepted the invitation."

"Oh, my gosh!" Aria screeched. "You are a terrible friend and sister."

"I'm saving you and I guarantee you will thank me later. Now, start thinking about what you're going to pack because you leave in eight days." Brandy passed Aria back her phone. "Aria, on a serious note. You should go. You have nothing to lose by going, but you can miss out if you stay. Life is too short to be miserable and being committed to a nigga that wants any and every bitch that's ready to lay on her back and spread her legs. This is the opportunity of a lifetime, so don't pass it up. And from the sound of y'all messages, there's some chemistry there."

Aria sat and stared at her phone for a while. Brandy was right. Life was about taking risks. It was the unknown that made it adventurous.

So, at that moment, she decided to take a chance and go on the trip. After all, what was the worst that could happen?

Chapter Two

Young Milli couldn't help but smile when Aria said she would seriously consider coming to the "A" to spend the Christmas holidays with him. Their ensuing telephone conversation only heightened his interest in her. *I like baby girl,* he thought as he moved around his luxurious 7-bedroom home getting ready to hit the streets.

It had been a minute since a female truly caught his attention. For the last three months, he had been pussy-free, meaning he hadn't fucked nothing, which was saying a whole lot because a nigga like himself had women literally throwing their panties at him 24/7, and not only when he was on stage performing.

Milli's growing popularity in the music industry paled in comparison to his street fame. Although he had just recently turned 27-years-old, he was considered a street veteran, being that he stepped off the porch at the tender age of eleven, caught his first body at fourteen, and made his first million dollars before he was legally old enough to buy liquor.

When a nigga had money, popularity, and hundreds of thousands of fans, not to mention good looks, women came a dime a dozen, and at times, Milli treated them as such. But his moms had raised him to recognize a good woman, and he thought he peeped that special gene in Aria.

"Time will tell. It always does," he said, recalling the foul shit his ex, Saliscia, did.

A rapper known as BNK, an acronym for *Bitch Nigga Killa*, had boasted in a song that he fucked Saliscia in the backseat of his Phantom, an allegation that turned out not to be entirely true. Still, the disloyal bitch had violated.

Milli slammed Saliscia against the living room wall of the condo he had leased for her. "Bitch, don't lie to me. This nigga on wax claiming he smashed your muthafuckin' stanking ass. That's how you rockin'? You fuckin' the opp?" His hand went around her throat and tightened.

"I. Did. Not. I swear!" She coughed out, barely able to breathe.

Milli ignored the tears pouring out of her deceitful eyes. That inner voice that controlled the beast in him told Milli to strangle the life out of the bitch, but he was too game-tight to throw away his freedom and everything he had earned over what a woman chose to do with her body.

Milli released Saliscia from his death grip. "You not even worth killing, shorty. I'ma let you live. But when I leave here you better fall to your knees and thank God I didn't give you what you deserve," he spat.

"Baby, I didn't fuck that fat ass nigga. I swear I wouldn't do you like that. All we did was talk. I can show you our text messages." Saliscia grabbed her phone off of the marble and glass table and scrolled through her texts until she found the proof she was looking for. "Here, this will prove to you he's lying." She extended the phone to Milli.

"I don't wanna see that shit!" He slapped the phone out of her hand, sending it crashing against the wall. "Fuck was you texting with that nigga for? You knew we were beefing and you all up in his car? Disrespecting my name in these streets? Bro, you better get the fuck outta my face before I body your ass!"

"I was hurt gotdammit! He showed me pictures of all these different hoes y'all use to fuck when y'all was cool. He had videos and everything. Videos that were made after you and I were together. I talked to him to get back at you! But I didn't go through with it. I never slept with him. I kissed him once.

Once! That's on God," Saliscia proclaimed. *"And then I felt sick to my stomach because I knew it was wrong and that I loved you despite what you did."*

"If you kissed another nigga, you might as well fucked him. It's all the same to me. What's mine no other nigga can touch, in any way. Matter of fact, when you entertained that fuck nigga it was the end of us. Period. Bitch!"

"Milli, please don't say that," she cried from deep down in her soul. *The thought that it was truly over between them felt like the end of her world.*

"You can write that shit in blood. It's a wrap." Milli grabbed his backpack off of the couch and retrieved $15,000 from inside. He tossed the large stack of bills at her feet. *"That's for whatever good you done while we were together. When I walk out the door you're dead to me."*

"Baby, please! I'm sorry. Let me make it up to you."

Milli ignored her pleas as he walked into the bedroom and grabbed the fits he had in her closet. By the time he reached the front door, Saliscia was holding on to the back of his shirt with every ounce of strength in her body. Milli's Gucci shirt ripped as he snatched away from her, leaving her crying on the floor of her doorway.

"Never again," he said before pulling off in his black on black Lamborghini.*

That was nearly nine months ago. For a minute, Saliscia had stalked Milli to the extent that he had thought he was gonna have to crush her like he had crushed many niggaz in the streets. But, eventually she backed off and word around Atlanta was that she was pregnant by BNK. Even now, Milli couldn't help but shake his head at that. It wasn't that he was heartbroken, but Saliscia's betrayal had definitely hurt his pride.

After Saliscia, it had been a stream of different females. Strippers, Instagram models, industry chicks and the likes. But Milli had been running up in different girls since his teenaged years and he was tired of that. He decided to test himself to see if he could forgo sex until he met a female that truly interested him. In the meantime, he dropped hot mixed tape after mixed tape and continued to get money in the streets by pushing major weed and pills. Now Aria was stirring up something in him that he thought was dead.

Money over bitches, he reminded himself. But all day long she remained on his mind.

Chapter 3

Saturday morning, Aria and Brandy linked up for breakfast and a trip to the mall. Milli sent her five-thousand dollars to shop with before her arrival. Ever since Brandy accepted the invitation for Aria to visit Milli, the two had been in constant contact. They would even Facetime when he was in the studio. Aria respected his love and dedication to his craft. It allowed her to see him behind the scenes.

Shoppers flooded the mall in search of Christmas gifts. Everyone was smiling and polite. The true display of Southern hospitality. It was something about this particular season that made humans cheerful.

"Girl, I am ready to go. My damn feet are killing me," Brandy complained as she clutched several shopping bags in her hand.

"This is the last stop and then we can leave." Aria and Brandy made their entrance into Victoria's Secret and to the back of the store.

Aria sifted through some sexy lingerie for the occasion. When she came across a one-piece black lace bodysuit and held it up. "What do you think?"

"It's cute, but you won't be wearing it for long."

"I don't plan to," Aria giggled, thinking about how their first encounter would go down.

"That's what I'm talking about, bestie. Pop yo' shit. I ain't gone lie that nigga look like he can tear a lining out the va-jayjay."

Both girls laughed. "I know, right? I swear I was thinking that," Aria agreed.

Brandy grabbed a sexy, red lace corset with matching panties and a garter. "You should get this one, too. I love it and I'm sure he will, too."

"That is cute," Aria agreed and grabbed the item from her hand. She glanced and it once before making her final decision. "We can leave now."

"I thought I would never hear you say that," Brandy sighed with relief. The malls were packed during the holidays and she hated it with a passion. She preferred to shop online and from boutiques on Instagram.

redOne hour later, they arrived back at Aria's house. On her way up the single step, Aria peeped a large brown box sitting on the porch.

"What you ordered?" Brandy asked.

"Nothing." Aria examined the box. Her name was on it, but she didn't recognize the name of the sender.

Aria unlocked the door, took her bags inside, and returned to grab the box. Once inside the home, she used a knife to open up the package and remove its contents. There was a card inside so she opened that first.

"Read it out loud." Brandy stood by impatiently waiting.

Seven days of Christmas.
I want you to fly in style, so enjoy the first of many gifts.
signed, Young Milli.

Aria held the card against her chest. Her wide smile heightened her cheekbones.

"Can you open the gift now? I'm anxious to see what he sent."

Aria opened up the package and was in awe. The beam in her eyes could light up the universe. Milli sent her a Louis Vuitton Horizon 55 rolling carry-on bag with the matching duffle bag. Aria was in love with the pink and blue tye dye effects of the luggage.

"Biiitch, I am in love. Look at this luggage," Brandy screeched with excitement.

"You're in love. I'm in love." Aria was equally excited. "I've been talking to this man for all of five minutes and this is the treatment I get. Jaheim ass never did no shit like this for me and I gave him two years."

"You can thank me now or later. It's up to you." Brandy was happy to see her best friend smile. It had been a while since she saw her smile that big. Aria deserved all of the happiness in the world.

"Not yet! I'm saving that for after this trip. If it turns out good, then I will. As of right now, it's all materialistic. He has a bag to blow, so it's no pressure on his end."

Truthfully speaking, Aria was smitten by his charm. And his presence made it easier to ignore Jaheim's weak-ass apologies. The gifts were a bonus. The way Milli treated her and made her feel would determine how she truly felt about him. In the meantime, she intended to enjoy her Christmas weekend with her social media crush.

Once Brandy left, Aria began to pack her bags. There was no sense in doing it last minute. Feeling lovely, she sipped wine from a tall glass and played soulful Christmas music. The anticipation of meeting with Young Milli in person had her antsy and excited. No one could ruin her mood. Well, almost no one.

A strong knock on the door interrupted her happy thoughts. Disappointment surfaced when she saw that it was Jaheim standing on her porch. Against her better judgment, she opened the door.

"What are you doing here, Jaheim?" Aria exhaled and rolled her eyes. His presence irritated every fiber of her being.

"I'm dropping off your keys as promised." Jaheim pushed his way inside and stood in the living room.

"You could've left them in the mailbox." Aria slammed the door behind him.

"I know, but I wanted to talk since the other half of your brain isn't present." Jaheim referred to Brandy with that slick remark.

"There's nothing for us to talk about. Our relationship is over and there is no coming back from what you did to me. Cheating is one thing, but a baby?" she shook her head. "I can't forgive you for that."

Jaheim moved closer and put his arm around her waist. Aria pushed him away, so he held his arms out and pleaded, shamelessly. "Come on, Aria. I fucked up, but that don't mean a nigga don't love you. Do you really think I give two fucks about that thot? It was a nut, nothing more, nothing less. Fa real, fa real, I don't even know that the baby is mine."

"Boy, you're pitiful." Aria shook her head in disgust.

"Nawl, I'm just keeping it a hunnid. Listen, baby," his eyes drooped and he effected a sad look across his face. "Why can't we sit down and discuss this like adults?"

"Because sadly, I'll be the only adult involved." Aria stood firm on her answer. There was no rekindling their relationship. It was over for real this time.

Jaheim spotted the expensive luggage and looked at Aria with a slight frown plastered on his face. "Where are you going?"

"Out of town."

"With who?"

"Why? It's not your concern."

"Yo' ma, stop playing with me. Where the fuck you going?"

Aria didn't want to get into an argument with Jaheim. All she wanted was for him to leave her key and go about his business, so she told him the half-truth. "I'm going to Atlanta to see my cousin for Christmas. I need to get away from here and clear my mind."

Jaheim gritted his teeth. He was heated that Aria hadn't shared the information with him prior to her making plans. "You know what, do that. Maybe that will give you some time to think about us and how we'll move forward in this relationship." Jaheim's demeanor changed instantly and he now wore a half-smile. "When you get back I'll have something planned for us, along with your Christmas gift." Jaheim pulled a key from his pocket and passed it to Aria. "I'll see you when you return. I love you and be safe. Don't make me have to come up there and act a fool." He kissed her forehead and walked out of the door.

Aria stood there in disbelief. Jaheim ignored everything she said while creating a different narrative in his head. He was delusional and the first thought in Aria's mind was to change the locks.

Jaheim left her feeling uneasy. The way he returned the key without a fight, led her to believe that he had no plans of leaving her alone. However, he was sadly mistaken if he thought their relationship would resume once she returned.

Aria picked up her glass of wine and cellphone. She needed to talk to someone that would take her mind off of the craziness in her life.

Chapter 4

After a productive day, during which he made $200,000 dollars from his street hustle, Milli capped it off by hitting the studio and laying down several new tracks that he planned to release soon. Now he was at home relaxing in his black marble bathtub, smoking a blunt of Pluto and sipping on a glass of Casamigos. His unreleased music video played from the television mounted on the bathroom wall.

That shit is cold, he said to himself. The producer had expertly captured the theme of the song titled *I Want All The Smoke*.

Through a haze of weed smoke, Milli saw his phone light up with an incoming call from Aria. A little gangsta smile enveloped his face. He answered the phone, putting it on speaker. "Hey, Melanin Queen. How you doing?"

"Awww, ain't you sweet. I'm doing okay, King. How was your day?" Aria blushed.

"Busy but prosperous. How about yours?"

"I don't want to bore you." Aria refused to share the drama that was going on between her and Jaheim. That was a part of her life Milli didn't need to know about. Sooner or later Jaheim would get the message and leave her alone.

"You could never do that. I find every little thing about you to be interesting."

"Really?"

"Facts," he reiterated, taking a pull from the blunt.

"I find that hard to believe," she said.

"Why is that? Don't you think you're interesting?" he asked.

"I do. But I'm sure you talk to so many women it's hard to differentiate one from the other."

"Nah, the cream always rises to the top. Besides, I'm not even moving like that. Excuse my realness, but most of these bitches out here are for any nigga that got a bag or a lil wave. I want something different. I deserve that," he said with certainty.

"I agree, and I'm definitely not one of those. I have my own. I'm sure it's nothing close to what you have but I'm not interested in you for your money."

"I know that, luv. I been checking you out on IG for almost six months and I've never seen you post anything thirsty," Milli acknowledged.

"That's because I'm not thirsty. Not even a tad bit. But I do want to thank you again for the shopping spree and for the luggage I just received from you. I hope you know you didn't have to do any of that."

"I know, but I wanted to make your day. Did I accomplish that?" he asked in a lowered, sexy tone.

"Yes, you definitely did. No one has ever done such nice, thoughtful things for me," Aria admitted as she stretched across her bed on her back, closed her eyes and pictured his thuggish, handsome face.

"Well, get used to it. And not just the gifts. I wanna make new memories with you every day, every hour, every minute we share. Whether it's on the phone, in a text or face to face," Young Milli crooned sincerely. His words caused Aria's breath to get caught in her chest.

After a moment of silence, she said, almost in a whisper, "Why me?"

"Because I like your vibe. My greatest strength in the world is my ability to read people. If I couldn't do that I would've been dead a long time ago. See I'm not an industry nigga, I'ma *in-da-streets* nigga. And in the streets, a man can't survive if he can't recognize the real from the fake."

30

"I wish I could do that," she replied, knowing how wrong she had been about men in the past.

Milli assured her that her judgment was just fine. "Most of the time the mistake is in the heart, not the mind." He spoke with a wisdom that belied his years.

For a minute, the mistakes she made with Jaheim played through her mind in a montage of regrets and foolish decisions. She had known a long time ago that Jaheim wasn't shit. But like Milli had said, she listened to her heart and not her mind. Those days were over, though.

With a backwards flip of her wrist, Aria dismissed Jaheim from her thoughts and listened to Milli expound further on what the streets had taught him. When he talked, his words were so descriptive they formed a movie in her mind. She could actually visualize every scenario he spoke of.

When the conversation shifted to his ex's betrayal, Milli didn't sound hurt or bitter. He sounded disappointed for Saliscia. Like, the biggest loss in it all was his respect for her. Aria felt that shit right there. Because that's how it was with Jaheim, she had no respect for him anymore.

When Milli spoke of the beef between him and BNK, something Aria had read about on social media, but she hadn't questioned him about it, hurt and anger jumped through the phone.

"It ain't even about what that clown ass nigga saying on social media. It's the fact that I'm the one who put him on. Bro came home from prison with nothing. Nada! Not a gotdam thing. I gave him a bag and a few hookups. Treated him like a brother from another."

By now, Milli was out of the tub, pacing back and forth in the spacious bathroom with a towel wrapped around his waist and the blunt hanging from the corner of his mouth.

Aria braved out a question. "Why did he turn on you?"

"Typical shit. Envy. Jealousy. See, no matter what bro gets, deep down he wanna be me. But I'm *one of one*. Ain't no other Young Milli's," he stated.

Aria heard that cockiness loud and clear, and it turned her the fuck on. Milli didn't come off like an arrogant A-hole, he was just stating his self-worth. And in the next breath he humbled himself.

"I digress, luv. I'm not even gonna allow bro no space in my head. That shit is beneath me. No matter what, I'm blessed. I'm chillin' at the crib, talking to a beautiful Queen who's coming to spend the holidays with me. What more can a man ask for?"

Aria had to stop herself from placing her hand between her thighs. Young Milli, without even trying, had her kitty purring. She took a few deep breaths to get it together. *Lord, I can't handle this man. He's going to have me floating on a cloud.*

Milli asked her to hold on while he answered an incoming call.

"Okay," said Aria, thankful for the break.

"Sup, fam?" Milli greeted the caller.

"Red alert! Number three."

"Say no more." Milli clicked back over to Aria. "Luv, I gotta call you back tomorrow. Something just came up."

"Is everything okay?" She could hear the change in his tone.

"Yeah, nothing is a problem if it has a solution. I'ma get back with you tomorrow," he repeated.

"Okay. Please be safe." Worry tinged her voice.

"I will. Bye."

Milli disconnected the call and headed straight to the bedroom to get dressed. Once he was adorned in all-black, with his ever-present bulletproof vest underneath his garb, he grabbed his Draco off of the dresser and slammed in a full clip. Some fools had ran up in one of his stash houses.

I guess I gotta remind these fuck niggas that I want all the smoke, he thought as he hurried out of the house and hopped into a nondescript vehicle that he kept in his garage for occasions such as this.

Before pulling out of his six-car garage, Milli commanded his voice-controlled sound system to play *When We Ride On Our Enemies,* an old Tupac song that matched his mood.

Come take a journey through my mind's eye
You crossed the game, don't explain, nigga, time to die
Say goodbye, watch my eyes when I pull the trigger
So right before you die, you bow before a bigger nigga

Some unlucky mothers would mourn their sons this Christmas.

Chapter 5

Per Milli's handwritten note inside of the box, the term, *seven days of Christmas*, had finally come full circle. Each day for the past week Aria received a gift from Young Milli. Aria felt special and wanted by a man. The way he pursued her was something she had never bared witness to in all of her years of dating.

Young Milli sent Aria a Birkin bag, a Dolce and Gabbana faux fur jacket with a pair of knee-high boots to match, and some cute oversized shades. And he didn't stop there. He also gifted Aria a Rolex watch and a custom diamond chain with her name on it from his personal jeweler.

To Milli, money was no object. It came and went. He cashed in on the daily and enjoyed spoiling the woman in his life. Aria wasn't his woman as of yet, but he planned on changing that narrative once he got to know her on a more personal level.

Their chemistry over the phone was electric and Aria was a beautiful sight for sore eyes. Aria was a woman of class, so he decided to take a different approach to her. It wasn't about the money with her and that's what made her more attractive in his eyes. Plus, he loved to see the smile on her face each time she thanked him.

Aria climbed from her king-sized bed and stretched her arms towards the ceiling. Her flight out to the "A" was scheduled to leave within the next few hours and she wanted to be on time.

Last night, while Aria was on the phone with Young Milli, she did an early check-in with Delta.

Aria took a hot shower, brushed her teeth, and moisturized her face and skin. Dressed in a pair of jeans and a top that exposed her belly button, Aria slipped her sized seven feet into the black leather D&G boots that Milli purchased. Quickly, Aria did a slight beat to her face and sprayed on some Versace perfume. Time was slipping away and she needed to get to the airport.

Brandy arrived at her house a little before eight that morning. Young Milli wanted her there early so they could spend the entire day together before night fell.

"Hey, boo. You smell good." Brandy backed out of the driveway.

"Thank you."

"You look cute, too. But you know it ain't cold enough for a damn faux fur coat, right?" Brandy snickered, but she was impressed with the way Young Milli was spoiling Aria.

"I know that, fool. I'm not putting it on until I land. Milli said it's cold and he wanted me dressed for the weather."

"I see," Brandy smirked.

Twenty minutes, later Brandy pulled into Delta's departure area at the Fort Lauderdale-Hollywood International Airport and put the car in park. Aria stepped out and retrieved her luggage, then she hugged Brandy.

"Thank you for being here for me through everything. Without you, none of this would've happened and I would've been lonely for the holidays."

"You don't have to thank me. You're my sister and I love you. Now, go and enjoy yourself, safely. Don't come back with no little Christmas miracle in your uterus, though."

"I am not getting pregnant, girl. Stop it!" Aria waved to Brandy as she made her way inside the terminal.

The checkpoint at the security station didn't take long at all. Within the next forty-five minutes, Aria was boarding her flight and seated in the first-class cabin. The view was astonishing and the level of comfort was incredible compared to economy. Aria had never experienced royal treatment like that before, but it was something she could get used to if things worked out between the two of them. Before take-off, Aria sent Young Milli a text.

Aria:9:15 a.m. We're about to take off.
Young Milli:9:16 a.m. Safe travels beautiful. I'll be waiting.

Aria passed on ordering food but did indulge in a glass of wine for the ninety-minute flight. She was on top of the world. Literally. By the time Aria finished her second glass of wine to settle the nervousness in her stomach, the pilot's voice came over the intercom alerting them that they were about to land. The landing was smooth and so was her trip to baggage claim. Aria walked through the airport and made her way to arrivals where Young Milli would be waiting.

The cold Atlanta air slapped her in the face as soon as she stepped outside into the sun. The shades she wore blocked the rays from blinding her sight, but it was a very bright morning still.

As promised Young Milli was sitting out front in his black 2021 Maserati Levante waiting for her. The caution lights blinked almost in sync wth Aria's pounding heart. She could not see him behind the dark, tinted windows, but it had to be him. Butterflies erupted in her stomach. Aria was nervous as hell. True enough they face-timed daily, but to her it wasn't the same. This was the moment of truth. She took a long, deep breath and asked the Lord to steady her legs.

***

Young Milli sat behind the wheel of his foreign whip, taking one last pull on a blunt. Smoke surrounded his head and filled the car with a strong but sweet aroma. The hardcore rap music that thumped from his high-quality Rockford Fosgate system was none other than his own.

Over the past year, he had become the hottest underground artist in the game. Although he was hotly pursued by all the major record labels, he preferred to remain on his own wave. *Why the fuck would I sign with a label and get paid pennies on the dollar?* he thought as he listened to his impeccable wordplay while recalling a seven figure offer he had rejected a few days ago.

Milli wasn't hard-pressed for money. Even though he had suspended all of his illegal dealings after the drama of a few nights ago, his net worth was still mind blowing. In the meantime, the sales from mixed tapes along with the revenue generated from the dozen or so properties and small businesses that he owned around Atlanta would continue to bring in bread.

It had been essential that he shut down his street pharmaceutical dealings for the time being because he expected heat from the po's. After his stash spot got robbed by known jackboys, Milli had responded with swift and lethal retaliation. Four mothers would have to bury their sons now and he expected the murders to draw unwanted attention from the cops. He had instructed every member of his team to chill until further notice.

In the middle of recalling how he emptied a full 30 round clip in two of the robbers, Milli looked up to see a ray of sunshine staring at his ride. He quickly sprayed some air freshener then slid out of the car. Even from more than twenty feet away

Aria's beauty and sexiness made his dick jump. She was wearing the short, chocolate mink jacket and the matching boots that he sent her a few days ago.

"That's a bad muthafucka," he said unconsciously.

Aria was having tiny heart attacks as he made his approach. She took in everything about him. His freshly oiled, blond tip dreads. The way he walked with a whole lot of natural swag. The jewels around his neck that swung side to side with each step he took. When he got closer, Aria saw that he was wearing a mink jacket that matched the color of hers. And damn if that nigga didn't have on what looked like matching mink socks!

"Why?" she smiled when he drew within arms-length of her.

"Why what?" He arched a brow.

"Nothing." Aria giggled. Milli was too much. In a really good way.

"Welcome to the "A", luv. How was your flight?"

"Thank you. It was wonderful."

"Good. Nothing but the best for a queen." He pulled her into an embrace that Aria didn't ever want them to break. His arms felt powerful and protective. And he smelled like heaven, touched with a hint of sin.

Aria inhaled his scent deeply. "Why are you doing this to me?" she asked innocently.

"I haven't done anything, yet. C'mon, let me get you out of this cold. The only time I want you to be icy is when I take you to Tiffany's," he said, reaching down to retrieve her luggage.

"I am not letting you take me to Tiffany's. Get that out of your mind, Milli. You've already spoiled me enough," she protested as she followed him to the Maserati.

Milli spun around and hushed her with a kiss. Aria thought she was going to float right up to the clouds. *This can't be real.* She wondered when she would wake up from this dream.

Milli placed her bags in the car then opened the passenger door for her. The air freshener had replaced the smell of weed inside the vehicle. The black and red leather interior was as soft as a baby's bottom. Milli walked around to the other side of the car and climbed in. He looked at her and smiled from his eyes to his mouth. In that moment, Aria knew that his attraction to her was genuine.

"You're finally here." He almost sounded amazed.

"I am." The truth was, Aria was more amazed than Milli.

"Well, get ready to have the best Christmas I can give you." He reached in the backseat, grabbed a red and white Santa's hat, and placed it on his head. "Call me Young Milli Claus."

Even though he looked ridiculous in the hat, Aria was loving it. As they drove away from the airport, she could only imagine what else he had in store for her.

Chapter 6

Another one of Young Milli's songs came through the speakers, but this particular song had an up tempo to it. Aria found herself nodding to the soft tunes about him rapping about having a down ass chick. Aria smiled at the thought of that chick being her. Every so often she would glance over at Young Milli with infatuation in her eyes and hunger in her heart. Aria wanted to be with a man that catered to her every want and need. Young Milli had a tough exterior, but on the inside he was sweet thus far. He was a rare breed and different from the man she saw on social media and read about in the blogs.

Young Milli caught Aria staring at him and returned the smile. No words were exchanged. They simply enjoyed the music and being in one another's presence for the thirty six minute drive to his mansion in Fayetteville. Young Milli pulled up to a luxurious home protected by a brick wall and black guard gate. Aria turned away when she saw him punch in a code on the key pad. It was private information and she didn't want to violate his personal information.

Young Milli pulled in front of the double French doors and killed the engine. Once he was out of the car, he stepped to the passenger side and opened her door like the gentleman he was. Aria placed her right foot out of the car and grabbed her purse. Just as she prepared to get out, Milli grabbed her hand.

"Aren't you a gentleman?" she blushed exposing the majority of her perfectly white teeth.

"Chivalry isn't dead, Queen. I'll always open doors for you. Literally and figuratively." Milli closed the door and grabbed her luggage.

"I like that."

Aria crossed the threshold of his immaculate home and once again she was impressed. Not only by the opulence but also at its cleanliness. It wasn't that she expected the interior to be a pigsty, but Milli was a young man, seven years younger than Aria, so she thought his place would resemble that of a bachelor. To her surprise, his home was fit for a wife and kids. Milli eyeballed Aria. She appeared to be tense.

"Welcome to my home. Make yourself comfortable. This is your home while you're here. Come on. Let me show you to the bedroom."

Aria tilted her head to the side. A slight smirk graced her pretty face. "Straight to the bedroom, huh?"

Her comment made Young Milli laugh. "Nah. It ain't like that. I want to show you where we'll be sleeping."

"I'm joking."

"I know," he replied smoothly. "Follow me."

Aria followed behind Young Milli and took in the scenery, along with the exquisite décor. She was impressed to say the least. As they stepped into the bedroom, Aria stopped in her tracks and looked around. The room was bigger than her living room and kitchen put together. And his bed was huge. It had to be the size of two king beds put together. Recently, she saw that rappers T.I and Quavo had the same type of bed. Aria guessed this was a new trend that the rich rappers started. There was no way he ordered the Versace sheets to cover it. He had to have those custom made.

"Why is your bed so huge?" She asked while moving closer and dropping her purse on top of it.

"I needed something fit for a king to lounge in and my queen to run on. If you know what I mean." Young Milli's voice was filled with heavy seduction, as he looked at her with lustful eyes.

Aria felt his words caress her skin and send a hot, tingling sensation between her thighs. Instantly, she visualized the two of them engaging in some hot and heavy sex in that very bed.

"I guess." Aria shrugged her shoulders to make it seem as if she was unfazed by his sexual remark and changed the subject. "Your home is really beautiful. I thought I was walking into a bachelor pad, but you proved me wrong."

"Looks like I'll be proving you wrong a lot." Young Milli picked up a long bag that was laid across his bed. "I ordered this for you. I hope you like it."

"Didn't I tell you not to buy me anymore gifts? I'm not interested in your money." Aria meant every word she said.

Young Milli invaded her personal space. He was so close that she could feel his breath on her skin. "Then tell me what you are interested in?"

"I'm interested in you. The type of man that you are." Aria made a bold move and placed her hand over his heart. "I want to know what's in here."

"In due time you'll find out."

"I hope so," she replied softly.

The two locked eyes for what seemed like forever. Aria could've sworn that she heard two hearts beating on one accord throughout the room. Once again, Aria's stomach fluttered with anxious butterflies. The chemistry was intense. Unadulterated animal attraction filled the air. Milli licked his lips. The gesture sent a bolt of lightning straight from Aria's eyes to her clit. Feeling weak in the knees, she hesitated on her next move, but it was hard to resist those luscious, soft lips.

Slowly, she moved forward and Milli met her halfway. This kiss was more passionate than the off guard one he planted on her at the airport. She was prepared for this one. Aria's hand remained on his chest, but Young Milli's hands found themselves gripping her curvy hips. Electricity flowed through Aria's body. His touch alone made her want to strip out of her clothes. To her discernment, Milli broke their kiss and took a step back. She frowned at him, but he paid her no mind.

"I have something special planned for you. So, I want you to freshen up and put on the dress that's in this bag. The bathroom is right there." Young Milli pointed towards the door.

"Okay." Aria grabbed the bag and sat it back on the bed. A hot shower was exactly what she needed thanks to the juices that she could feel against her thighs.

Milli sat on the edge of the bed and watched Aria strip down to her panties and bra. She had the body of a black Venus, the goddess of love and beauty. Her legs were long, smooth and shapely, and her small waist flared out into hips that promised the ride of a lifetime. He stole a quick look between her thighs and saw a plumpness that made his mouth water.

"Close your mouth," she teased. "Be good and you just might get a taste of ecstasy."

"Oh, you talking shit now, huh?" he chuckled.

"Maybe. Just a little." Aria stuck her tongue out at him, then turned and headed for the bathroom.

"I'ma do more than taste it. And when I do, don't run."

"Me? Run? Now why would I do that," she said over her shoulder just before going into the bathroom and closing the door behind her, bringing an abrupt end to Milli's peep show.

He smiled and stroked his hardened pole through the fabric of his pants. He knew he really liked Aria, but he couldn't believe how much she turned him on. He wanted to go into the shower and ravish her, pin her to the wall and stamp his name on that ass. But he also wanted to take his time with her and let things happen organically.

As Milli waited for Aria to emerge from the bathroom, he made a quick call to let his security team get in place. "What you riding in today, boss man?" asked Damu, the chief of security.

"The stretch. Have K-dog drive. I want you and Mob Slim to follow us in separate cars. I'm not taking anything for granted. I'm tryna show my lady friend a good time and with everything going on in the streets and on IG, ain't no telling who may try to step."

"Already," said Damu, a certified hitter who had moved to Atlanta from Compton, California a few years ago. He and Milli had met through a mutual friend and formed a strong bond.

"Pull up. We'll be ready."

Milli decided to use one of the other eight bathrooms to freshen himself up and to change into a different fit, something that didn't smell of weed.

A short while later, he and Aria met back up in his bedroom. Aria could tell from Milli's expression that she was rocking the hell out of the dress he wanted to see her in. His eyes told her that to him she was all that. She felt the sexiest she had ever felt in her life. Milli looked *scrumdiddlyumptious,* too. If the heavens above allowed her one taste of him, Aria figured that this life wouldn't owe her nothing else.

She covered her mouth with a hand to stop herself from giggling at the thought.

"Sup, luv?" Milli raised an inquisitive eyebrow at her.

"Nothing." Aria feigned innocence.

"Well, why you over there acting like Celie from *The Color Purple?*"

"Shug like honey. And now, I's just like a bee," she mocked, quoting a popular line from the classic movie.

Milli cracked up. He laughed so hard he made Aria burst out in laughter, too.

45

"You stoopid," he said, wiping tears from his eyes.

Aria loved his laughter. She knew that men like Milli rarely got the opportunity to laugh real hard, deep from the gut. Too often life forced them to wear a scowl. It was like a bullet proof vest to protect them from the everyday bs that came their way. She told herself that as long as she shared his company, she would try to add laughter and smiles to his life. It was the least that she could do for someone who so generously gave to her.

They joked back and forth as she watched Milli drape himself in expensive jewels, including his *YM* nameplate chain, an icy bracelet and a Patek Philippe watch on the opposite wrist. Being a fashion geek, Aria recognized the high-end brands that her knight in shining armor wore. He accentuated it all with a few light dashes of Louie V cologne. Then, he patted his chest to make sure he had on his bpv, grabbed his Glock off of the nightstand and tucked it in his waist. *Just in case an opp slips by my goons.*

Now he felt safe and ready to show the Queen the city.

Chapter 7

When they stepped out of the front door, the Cadillac Escalade stretch limo was already parked in the circular driveway, close to the house. Towering at 6'8", and weighing 320 lbs, K-dog, the chauffeur, was an imposing figure, dressed in black and wearing dark shades. Aria had to strain her neck to look him in the face. Her eyes went from him to the long, white limo that seemed to stretch a whole city block.

"You think we have enough room," she deadpanned as they climbed into the backseat of the 14-passenger luxury vehicle.

"Get used to it, baby girl. I do everything big. You only live once," Milli explained.

"Hush. I'm definitely not complaining." She leaned over and touched her lips to his.

"That's all I get? A peck?"

"You can get whatever you want," she paused dramatically, "but later."

"Promise?" he asked.

"Promise," she replied.

"Whatever?" He gave her a sly grin.

"I'ma get back with you on that," Aria said, allowing herself an out in case Milli was into bondage or some other crazy shit. She was feeling him but he'd better not expect nothing weird.

They began their day by having lunch at Poor Calvin's restaurant. Young Milli swore by the bible that they had the best lobster mac and cheese in Atlanta. That had Aria anxious to try it for herself. Along with her lobster mac and cheese, she ordered a mixed salad and a glass of Cabernet Sauvignon.

Milli had a half lobster tail, tiger shrimp and rice, and a glass of the same delicious wine Aria ordered.

"So, how was the food?" Milli asked once they were back in the limo.

"I must admit that it was good. I guess you have good taste."

"No doubt about that. I chose you, didn't I?" Milli stated with supreme confidence.

"I can't argue with that," Aria blushed

"So, what would you like to do next?"

"I would love to visit Tyler Perry Studios."

"Sayless."

Young Milli instructed K-dog to take them to the next destination. As they pulled off he checked to make sure the other cars were in position.

In route to the studio, Aria moved closer to Milli. He draped his arm across her shoulder and rubbed her arm. Aria closed her eyes and enjoyed the ride.

At the studio, they spent a little over an hour holding hands and navigating through the crowd. More than a few people recognized Young Milli and asked him to pose for a picture. Aria stepped to the side and allowed him to interact with his fans. She found his humbleness attractive, and she was pleased that he wasn't an arrogant ass like some celebrities. That would've been a complete turn off.

Watching Milli interact with a couple of young girls, who were in full blown groupie mode, did nothing but strengthen Aria's respect for him. At no time did he exhibit any interest in the star struck females, beyond being polite to them. Aria could tell that both girls had gotten their bodies done, but she wasn't intimidated by their super big asses and incredibly small waists. After all, she was naturally a stunna.

Milli walked back over to Aria and put his arm around her waist. "Sorry, baby. This happens when I go out in public. If it bothers you I can just tell them I'm out with my lady and I'm not taking any pictures today."

"No, boo. I don't mind at all. Get your shine on." Her understanding was music to his ears.

After they left Tyler Perry Studios, they slid by the Trap Music Museum. That was another place that she wanted to visit. Aria loved that Milli had no qualms about taking her anywhere she wanted to go. They even held hands until it was time to take pictures. Aria had Milli snapping photos of her in the trap kitchen, holding bricks and a Pyrex. A few fans wanted pics with Young Milli, he agreed and had them to snap a few photos of him and Aria together. Aria felt like a celebrity herself. Young Milli kept staring at her like she was that dessert he had wanted at Poor Calvin's.

Milli indeed couldn't take his eyes off of her for long. The way the sweater dress fit her body like a glove had him stuck. When he ordered it for her, he knew she would kill it. Now, he couldn't wait to take it off of her.

As the evening hues encompassed the city, they ended up at a popular night club. Apparently, it was his go to spot because Aria could remember seeing him posting pictures of him at the same club. Young Milli and Aria were escorted to a private VIP section, followed by Damu and the other two hittas. The staff treated them all like royalty. Aria observed one of the waitress' maneuvering through the crowd holding up a bottle with a sparkler coming out of it. She walked into the VIP section and sat the bottle down in front of Milli. He tipped her and sent her on her way.

"Let the turn up begin." Milli fixed a cup of Casamigos and passed it to Aria.

"I'm ready for it."

The music was banging, the crowd was lit, and plenty of ballers were in attendance. Model-like chicks outnumbered the men three to one. Aria thought she spotted Da Baby to the left of them and The Migos to the right. A couple of other well known rappers came over to their table and gave Milli some dap. Other men who appeared to be d-boys to Aria's trained eyes came over and paid their respects. It was obvious that Milli had major clout.

As the evening drew on, the DJ called Young Milli to the stage to do an impromptu performance. Milli didn't hesitate or disappoint. He had the club turnt. The way he electrified the crowd was something to behold. On stage his magnetism was through the roof. From the booth, Aria eyed him seductively when he took off his shirt. Even though he had on a bulletproof vest, the defined muscles in his shoulders and arms attested to him having a rock hard chest. Every female in the building was screaming his name. Aria was unbothered because she knew who he was leaving with.

The alcohol rocked her system and she was ready to get back to the house. Young Milli had threatened her with a good time in the bedroom one too many times today, and she desperately wanted to see if he could turn her into a track star.

Out of the corner of her eye, Aria spotted a group of men enter VIP. Something about their presence unnerved her. They seemed to have a palpable effect on the energy inside of the club. When they posted up, Aria recognized one of them. It was BNK. He was looking at the stage, mugging her boo with a hatred thick enough to cut with a knife. Aria, sobered up quickly. Her heart pounded against her chest. Had they come there to confront Young Milli? she worried.

A millisecond after the thought came to mind, she saw all three of Milli's goons get up from their table and approach

BNK. She couldn't hear what any of them were saying but their body language was worrisome. This was a part of the rap game that concerned Aria.

A rapper named Young Dolph had recently been murdered in his hometown of Memphis, Tennessee. His death was just one in a long line of deadly violence in the industry. Immediately, she feared for Young Milli's safety. She didn't have to, though. Milli was on point.

Chapter 8

After his electrifying performance, Milli hopped off of the stage, put his shirt back on and made his way back to the VIP area. Having spotted BNK and his weak ass entourage of internet gangstas, Milli moved with the stealth of a black panther. The fierce expression on his face as he neared their table made Aria uneasy. He looked ready to bang. The last thing she wanted was for him to get himself in any trouble, so she stood up to intercept him.

Aria couldn't get a word out of her mouth before Milli moved her aside.

"Sit back down." His tone was commanding and left no room for her to challenge him. So she sat.

Milli walked over towards BNK and his crew. A few bodies parted and he went nose to nose with the friend who had turned foe. "Sup, blood?" Milli challenged.

"What you mean?" BNK was trying not to shrink in front of his crew.

"Fuck that, nigga. Let's make these thangs pop." Milli's hand was up under his shirt.

BNK was surprised that Young Milli was packing heat. The doorman hadn't allowed BNK and his boys to bring their guns inside. Knowing better than to bring fists to a gunfight, BNK wisely deescalated the conflict, but anger shone in his eyes. "Bro, it ain't even like that. We're just out to have a good time. I'm meeting my AR here. Don't nobody have to die tonight."

Milli cocked his head slightly and studied BNK's facial expression. The look on his mug told Young Milli that he was backing down now, but would bring the drama to him later, when the odds weren't against him. That inner beast started whispering inside Young Milli's head. *Don't let this nigga walk away and come back for you another day. Clap his bitch ass. Right here. Right now.*

A younger Milli might've did just that. But this version of himself was wiser. Besides, he had shooters to handle this type of shit. Without saying another word, Milli turned and walked back over to Aria. Everyone in VIP breathed a collective sigh of relief.

Milli assured Aria that everything was good. It took a minute for her to get back in a party mood, but when she saw him relax, she relaxed, too. Milli had calmed down but he kept one eye on Aria and the other on the opp. His hittas weren't drinking or partying. They were locked in and focused. Damu placed a call to the homies and thirty minutes later, two dozen reinforcements showed up. Now Milli could give Aria his full attention again.

Now that the atmosphere was back to normal, Milli and Aria recaptured the heat that existed between them. Aria's hormones were getting the best of her. Images of Young Milli performing onstage truly had her hot and bothered. She was ready to feel him. Even the way he had commanded her to sit down had her dripping wet.

"Can we go?" she asked.

"Yeah, I'm ready to feel your head on my chest." He stroked her face with the back of his hand.

"Mmmm," she savored his touch.

In the limo, filled with liquor courage, Aria slipped her leg over Young Milli's lap and kissed his lips. He reciprocated and slid his tongue into her mouth. The passion in the backseat was thick enough to fog the windows. Aria could feel moisture soaking her panties. Her body craved this man's touch so bad that she was about to lose it. She wasn't concerned about the driver. His best bet was to keep his eyes on the road. Aria anxiously felt around for Milli's hand. Once her fingers grazed his wrist, she grabbed his hand and placed it in between her legs.

Milli couldn't resist her advances if he wanted to. He could feel the heat brewing underneath her dress and the wetness on his fingers.

She ready, ready, he thought to himself.

Milli caressed her kitty then pulled her panties to the side before easing two fingers into her hot box. Aria's hips moved gracefully to the pace of his hand, as he pushed in and out.

He pulled his fingers from Aria's spot and rolled up the middle window for some privacy.

"Keep going," Aria mumbled against his lips.

Milli obliged and placed his fingers back inside of her warm pussy. His dick was pressed hard against the fabric of his pants and he was ready to smash. They couldn't make it home fast enough. When the stretch finally came to a complete stop. Milli looked up and realized they were back at his house. Abruptly, he removed his fingers. Aria opened her eyes and watched him suck her juices from his hand.

"We're home. Come on." To K-dog, he said, "I'ma get back with y'all tomorrow."

Aria stripped out of her clothes and boots as soon as she made it into the room. She was wearing the sexy lingerie that she bought from Victoria's Secret underneath.

Milli dimmed the light then began to get undressed himself. When he was down to nothing but his boxer briefs, he walked over to the bed where Aria stood waiting nervously. "Don't get scared now," he said, feeling her eyes glued on the massive tent below his waist.

Aria swallowed hard. "I'm not scared," she half-lied. She was indeed scared and also anxious. It looked like he would split her in two but she was ready to give it a try.

"Come here, pretty lady." He pulled her close against his inked chest, tilted her head up, and covered her mouth with his. As their tongues did a tango, he palmed her ass roughly, like a man that knew she was his.

Aria slid her hand inside of his boxers and encircled his throbbing hardness. His length and thickness had her damn near traumatized. The head of his dick was big and round, shaped like a fireman's hat. *Oh my God!* Aria wasn't sure if he could fit inside her tight na na, but she was damn sure gonna find out.

She took him out and stroked him, slowly. Milli grew even larger. The desire to wrap her lips around his manhood was uncontrollable. As if he could read Aria's mind, Milli whispered, "Do your thing, luv."

Aria had longed for this moment all day, so she wasn't going to be shy. She was a grown woman, in the arms of a nigga who made her feel special in every way. She wanted to show him how special she could make him feel. She slid his boxers off and sunk to her knees, kissing the head of his dick while making soft moans. She locked around that beautiful bulb and then up and down the length of him. When she took him inside of her mouth, it was Milli who moaned.

"Fuck!" he said in a tone that inflamed her passion.

"You like that, bae?" She looked up at him with erotic eyes.

"Fuck yeah." Milli placed his hand in the back of her head.

"Watch me while I suck this dick," she cooed as she began to put it on his young, sexy ass.

Aria bobbed up and down on that meat, wetting it with lots of spit. She used both hands to jack him while her hot mouth made him feel like the top of his head was about to explode. Milli rose up on the tips of his toes, trying to run from her neck game. Aria was lethal with that shit. She slid one hand down to his balls and gently cupped them. Feeling brave, she took him deeper and deeper inside her mouth until she gagged. She pulled back a little then stepped back to her business.

That head action and loud slurping had Milli seeing martians. What Aria could do with her mouth should've been a first class felony. He was on the verge of busting a fat ass nut, but he wanted to save that for an even warmer place than her mouth. He tried to pull Aria up to her feet, but she wasn't having it. She wanted to see what that nut tasted like.

"Un uh," she protested.

Fuck it, Milli said to himself. He was young and vibrant. He could rock back up in a heartbeat. He placed his hands back on the top of her head and rode the wave.

Aria didn't just suck the dick, she swallowed that huge muthafucka. When she felt him swell in her mouth, she applied more pressure by caressing his nutsac. Feeling sexy and nasty, she dripped spit on that long, thick pole, and then slopped it back up.

Gangsta ass Young Milli damn near squirmed like a bitch, but the sounds he made were deep and full of base. "Suck it, baby," he said. "Do that shit! Oh, yeah, I'ma give it to you."

Aria wanted it. Needed it. Needed to know that she could give him untamed bliss. "Cum in my mouth, bae," she said, as she sucked him from tip to base.

Milli couldn't hold back. "Arggghhh!" he growled, as he unleashed his load.

Aria tried to catch and swallow every drop, but his nut was too plentiful. Some ran down from the corners of her mouth. She caught that with her tongue and showed it to him.

Milli's eyes were half-closed but he saw her. She had damn near sucked the life out of him. "Bet that," he said on weak breath. "Now your ass is in trouble. Let's see if you can take it like you give it."

Chapter 9

Aria kept her eyes on Milli as she removed her panties and bra, slow and seductive like a stripper. In another life, she could be an exotic dancer. Backing up slowly, she positioned herself on the bed and waited anxiously for the pain and pleasure Milli was about to inflict upon her body. Shamelessly, she spread her legs and gently rubbed her clit getting herself more aroused than she already was. Milli watched with satisfaction while stroking his limp pole in an effort to awaken the beast.

Milli stepped to the bed and gripped Aria's thighs with his forearms, pulling her closer to him. Aria closed her eyes and took a deep breath. The stroke of his warm, long tongue forced sensual moans to escape her full lips. "Ahh! Ooh!" she moaned.

Aria's back hit a high arch when he latched down on her swollen pearl and sucked on it. It sent multiple chills up her spine. His tongue moved in between her folds before penetrating her spot. She just knew that he was tracing his name all over her ovaries.

"Mmm. Mmm," she moaned slightly while clenching a hand full of his dreads.

Young Milli munched down on her goodies like it was his dessert that he missed out on earlier. Heavy slurps filled her ears. The juiciness from her twat made it easy for Milli to insert two fingers. Rapidly, he slid his fingers in and out, while catching every drop she released without an orgasm. When it became too much for Aria, she clamped his head in between her legs to stop the tongue lashing he applied to her gentle jewel.

"Wait! Wait!" she pleaded.

Milli ignored her pleas and didn't hesitate to forcefully push them apart and hold them against the mattress. Aria's moans heightened and turned into heavy, throaty moans. Her grip on his dreads grew tighter. "Baby! Baby! Don't stop. I'm about to cum."

Once those words invaded his ears, Milli stopped abruptly sending her into a frenzy. He didn't want to risk Aria tapping out too early. Standing tall and hard like the Statue of Liberty, he rubbed his dick against her plump lips before pushing in between her delicate petals. Aria clenched her muscles and butt cheeks as he stretched her wide open and filled her up inch by inch. She lost her breath when Milli used his arms to hold her legs open and beat it up. The liquor had him on go and he had to punish her for that slick talk.

Aria bit down on her lip and gripped his waist to try and guide his pace, but that didn't work. He was applying that pressure. For a moment, she could've sworn she felt her body elevate off of the mattress like the chick from the exorcist.

"Milli. Milli," she panted heavily. "Shit." Aria squirmed underneath his solid frame. She was trying to level the playing field.

"Nah, don't run. Take all this dick," he demanded.

"I can't. You killing me," she whined. He had officially turned her into a believer. Aria held her breath when he put her legs on his shoulders. From her diaphragm, she released a loud wail. Milli was nailing her to the cross and killing her stomach in the process. It felt like she was getting hit in both holes at once. Aria reached for things on the bed that weren't there, so she gripped the sheets instead.

Milli dropped her legs and kissed her in the mouth. "Turn over," he instructed.

Aria positioned her knees and elbows on the mattress and arched her back. Milli glided his inches deep within her walls and went to pound town. He was focused on catching that nut. In between thrusts, he smacked her on the ass. Aria held her head back when she felt Milli grip her long plaits. Forcing her head back further, he leaned forward and sucked on her lips. The intensity of his thrusts sent sharp pains to her bladder. It hurt, but yet it felt so good.

Aria eased her right hand in between her legs and fondled her clit. Milli spit down the crack of her ass and slipped his finger into her Hershey highway, causing Aria's eyes to roll to the back of her head. An orgasm was on the rise. Her body started to shake uncontrollably. The friction from her fingers going to work and Milli penetrating both holes led to a catastrophic, heavy release.

Moments later, Milli shook violently as he released an immense amount of soldiers into her body.

Milli pulled out and laid on his back. Aria joined him and laid her head on his chest. "I see your ass ran," he chuckled.

"Well, just call me Flo Jo then cause you did that." Aria released one final moan and rubbed his chest. "My legs hurt and all. It feels like I just ran a damn marathon."

"Shit, the way you sucked a nigga soul out his body I owed you a punishment."

"Lesson learned," she giggled." Aria and Young Milli snuggled up under one another until they drifted off to sleep.

The following morning, Aria extended her arm to reach for her king in hopes of a round two. Milli was like a strong cup of Folger's coffee and she needed him to start the day. To her disappointment, he wasn't there. Tossing the covers off of her naked body, Aria climbed out of bed and made her way into the bathroom to relieve herself. She had been holding her pee all night long and she was about to explode.

When she returned to the bedroom, Milli was standing in the middle of the floor dressed in a pair of grey sweatpants and a wife beater looking sexy as hell. Aria's mouth salivated the second she locked eyes with the bulge in his pants.

"Look who decided to wake up with the rest of the world." Aria stepped into his arms and placed her lips onto his for a pop kiss. "You was snoring your ass off," he chuckled playfully.

"I was tired." Aria wrapped her arms around his waist and pressed her body against his. "That's because somebody wore me out last night." Easing her hand into his cotton pants, she caressed his rod through his boxers. "I'm ready for round two."

"I would love to, but I can't right now. I'm having a meeting downstairs with the team."

"How long?" she whined with her lip poked out.

"It won't be too long." Milli touched her bottom lip with his thumb. "Stop pouting before I find you something to do with these pretty muhfuckas," he threatened.

His aggressiveness sent a signal straight to her vagina. "You sure you can handle that?"

"Oh, you talking big shit early in the morning," he smirked deviously. "That ain't what you was saying last night when you tried to hit the hundred yard dash across my mattress." Milli caressed her bare ass cheeks with both hands. "You sure you wanna start the day out tired?"

"The best part of waking up is dick up in your guts!" Aria sang out her response, causing him to laugh out loud.

"Yo' you say some of the craziest shit. I swear, but I love it. You keep a nigga laughing."

"I'm here to bring joy and peace. I don't like to battle with my man." Aria caught herself staking claims on Young Milli. Quickly, she cleaned it up. "I mean, I don't like to battle when I'm in a relationship with a man."

"I'm your man, huh?" he asked in a deep, sexy tone.

"You know what I mean."

"Yeah, daddy dropped that meat last night and bae is hooked." Milli grinned, stroking his ego and her pussy lips, too.

His tender touch alone made Aria's body tremble. She looked into his eyes and bit down on her lip. "Don't start nothing you can't finish."

Milli removed his hand and sucked his fingers. "I always finish what I start. You should know that by now. Anyway, let me get back to this meeting. I just wanted to see if you were awake."

"Okay. I'm about to take a shower."

"Nah. Wait for me. I won't be long. I promise."

"Okay."

Aria flopped down on the bed and grabbed her cellphone to call her bestie. Since her arrival, she hadn't checked in with Brandy or responded to the text she received last night.

"Well, look who decided to call me after being away for almost twenty-four hours," Brandy teased.

"I know, sis. My bad. I was supposed to call you once I landed." Aria crawled underneath the cover.

"Soo, how is it going with my new brother-in-law?" Brandy was sitting at her kitchen table drinking a cup of coffee.

Aria giggled at the thought of being in an exclusive relationship with Young Milli, one of the most desirable men in the industry. The drama that came along with the industry and their many hoes could easily kill a relationship. She had seen it too many times in the blogs. But when it came down to Milli and the way he carried himself as a man, it was a risk she was willing to take. Aria gave her bestie a complete rundown of their first date and sexual encounter.

After spending thirty minutes on the phone, laughing and giggling, they said their goodbyes. It was then that she decided to hit up her little cousin, Simona, that resided in Atlanta.

"Hey, Aria. What's up, girl?"

"Hey. I was calling to let you know that I'm in Atlanta for Christmas and I wanted to see you."

"Oh, okay. That's cool. What you doing up here?"

"Well, my friend invited me up here to celebrate the holidays with him, so here I am."

Simona cut her eyes at the cellphone screen as if Aria could see the look of shock and curiosity on her face. "What damn friend? What happened to Jaheim?"

"Girl, he messed up one time too many." She gave Simona a quick recount of Jaheim's betrayal.

"He's a dog ass nigga for that. I'm glad you stopped dealing with his grimey behind," scoffed Simona. "So, who's your new boo?" She piped up.

"Young Milli."

"Young who?" Simona screeched and snatched up her phone. "I know I'm not hearing shit. Did you just say *Young Milli*? Like the rapper Young Milli?"

Simona's star struck reaction had Aria cracking the hell up. "Yes. The rapper Young Milli."

"The fine-ass rapper *Young Milli*?" Simona wouldn't stop asking the same question repeatedly.

"Yes, girl. Calm down."

"Hell nah! How did you meet that nigga? Like give a bitch some tea or something."

"I met him on Instagram. We follow each other and he started hitting me up in my DM and here we are." Aria gave a brief rundown. "Would you like to meet him?"

"*Would I?* Hell yeah! I want a picture for Instagram, too." Simona jumped up and down with a big smile on her face.

"Okay, we're going out tonight. I'll send you the details and you can meet us there."

"Cool. Thank you, cousin."

"You're welcome. I'll see you later."

"You surely will."

Another hour had passed before Milli made his way back into the bedroom. By this time, Aria was locked in on the television that was built into the wall, catching up on Tyler Perry's show Ruthless. Playfully, he hopped onto the bed, straddling her and planted tender kisses all over Aria's face.

"You was lonely without me?"

"Yep!"

"Aww! You missed daddy."

"I surely did." Aria appreciated the playful side to Milli and the way he openly displayed his affection towards her. He made her feel like a woman and a friend. It felt like she'd known him for years. Aria could feel his stiffening pole resting on her thigh. The vibration between her legs had her ready to jump into round two.

"You going to the studio with me? You can watch me work."

"Of course."

"You still naked under here?" Young Milli licked his lips.

"And you know it."

"Come on. Let's take a shower."

Chapter 10

Young Milli stripped out his clothes and vest, and stepped into the marble walk-in shower with Aria directly on his heels. Heat filled the air and steam fogged the glass, but that wasn't the only thing heating up behind closed doors. Aria straddled Milli's lap as he sat on the ceramic bench, and eased down partially onto his massive wood since she hadn't fully adjusted to his size. Locking her mouth with his, Aria gradually moved up and down his shaft.

Milli broke their kiss and placed his right hand around her throat. "Nah, bae, you gotta ride all this dick." He sucked on her bottom lip and forced her down until he fully disappeared inside of that fat pussy. Aria's loud moan was partially suppressed by his mouth. Her body tensed up immediately.

"Ride that dick," he whispered in between his manly grunts. "Yeah, bae. Just like that."

Aria rode Milli until she felt him lift her up in his arms and pin her against the wall. The slip resistant porcelain tile made it easy for him to beat her down without falling. Milli rammed every inch in the kitty and stamped his name all over her. The water had his body glistening, as it trickled down his firm chest. Aria kept her arms tightly around his neck out of fear of falling, while her back slid up and down the cold tile.

"Fuck. Bae. Shit." She bit down on the side of his neck and sucked on his skin. Milli had the type of dick that would make a woman pack up her whole life in a U-Haul and follow his lead.

Aria snapped out of her daydream when she heard Milli grunting. "Fuck! I'm about to bust all in this pussy."

She had no intentions on getting pregnant, but she never told him to pull out either. Nor did she suggest that he wear a condom. She knew that she was living on the edge, but Milli had her wide open. After a few more grunts and groans, he let her down gently to the floor. Her legs wobbled the second her feet hit the tile.

They had worked up an appetite, so after getting dressed they headed out on the town to grab some food. They ended up at Twisted Soul, a soul food restaurant. Aria was in the mood for something heavy and good. She had the southern marinated fried chicken, mac and cheese, sweet potato chutney and collard greens. Young Milli had oxtails, rice, and black-eyed peas. To drink, Milli stuck with Casamigos, and Aria tried her hand at a mixed cocktail called, No Cryin' At The PYNK. The drink was named after the popular television show P Valley on Starz.

After their meal, they made it back inside the limo and that was when Aria thought about her cousin, Simona. She held Milli's hand in hers. "Bae, I spoke to my cousin today and I was wondering if you mind her tagging along at the studio and to the lounge with us tonight. I really want to see her and plus, she's a big fan of yours." Aria wanted to lay it on thick just in case he wasn't feeling the idea.

"That's cool. I don't mind."

"Thank you. She's going to be so happy." Aria kissed his cheek and pulled out her cellphone.

"Whatever makes you happy," he assured her. "Do we need to pick her up?"

"Can we?"

"Yeah. Get the address."

"Okay."

Aria called Simona and got her address. Milli instructed K-dog to make a detour from the studio.

Within thirty minutes they were pulling up to some apartments twenty minutes away from the restaurant. When K-dog opened the door for Simona to get in she lost all of her marbles. She was jumping up and down and forgot all about Aria the second she saw Young Milli.

"Oh, my God!" she screeched. "You are my favorite rapper in the whole world and I can't believe that I'm this close to you." Simona had her phone out and ready to show out for social media. "You have to take a picture with me so I can post it on my page." Simona's mouth moved faster than late-night traffic on I-75 North. Aria had to calm her down.

"Simona, relax," she giggled.

"It's cool. I love all my fans," said Young Milli.

He took a few photos with Simona during the ride to the studio.

Upon their arrival, Milli's security detail escorted them up to the fourth floor of a glass building and into a private suite with a lot of high tech electronics. Milli made sure Aria and her cousin were comfortable before he stepped inside the booth to do his thing.

Throughout his session, a few well-known rappers showed up to drop a verse on the new album he was working on. Aria recognized them, but only spoke when she was spoken to. The betrayal between BNK and Milli's ex was enough for her to be less social as possible. There was no need for her to be skinning and grinning in another man's face. First and foremost, she wasn't a groupie and secondly, she had the man that she wanted.

Simona on the other hand was star struck and thirsty and it showed. Aria understood that she was only twenty-six, but she truly wanted her cousin to stop embarrassing her.

Milli spent two hours in the booth and another hour turning up with the rappers on his track. Thick clouds of smoke filled the room and bottles were being passed around. Aria sat close to Milli and sipped on her drink. They were lit on Instagram live and posting pictures. Simona even twerked on one of their lives.

Thirty minutes later, the bottles were empty and his boys were ready to head out to 2chainz lounge Escobar.

The line was packed when they pulled up, but Young Milli and his crew didn't have to wait to get in. They were taken inside and escorted to their section that was blocked off with blue velvet ropes. Milli and his crew ordered several bottles of different liquor, brown and white. Milli ordered a hookah for Aria and Simona. The DJ had the place jumping. A group of girls were in the corner twerking and drinking straight out the bottle. Milli shook his head in amusement and turned back to Aria who seemed to be enjoying herself. Her demeanor had changed since the studio and she was now dancing along with her cousin. The DJ played Young Milli's latest single and that had him crunk. He stood behind Aria rapping and holding a bottle of liquor in his hand, while she twerked on him.

Moments later, Aria excused herself to go to the bathroom. She didn't want to interrupt Simona who was turnt. "I'm going to the restroom. I'll be right back," she yelled over the music.

"I'm coming with you," said Milli.

Damu stepped in and stopped Milli from leaving their section. "I got her. You don't need to be walking through the crowd."

"A'ight," he agreed and sat down so he could wait on Aria to return. He watched as Damu ushered her through the crowd of partygoers.

Simona danced her way into Milli's direction and sat down beside him. It was a little too close for him, but he brushed it off as her being overexcited. Simona scanned the area to see if anyone was looking, but everyone was busy turning up. She placed her hand on Milli's chest and licked her lips. "What you doing over here by yourself looking bored?"

"I'm coolin'. Sup?" Milli pushed her hand away.

"I hope this doesn't sound rude but a boss nigga like you need a young, pretty bitch like me on his arm. Aria is too old for you."

"I'm good." His brows knitted, but that didn't deter Simona. She offered to hook up with him later.

"Aria doesn't have to know. I can keep a secret," she added.

"You buggin'."

Simona decided to switch tactics. She wanted to get him on the dance floor and back that ass up on his dick. Give him a sample of what she had to offer. "Young Milli, do you want to dance?" she asked.

"Nah! I'm straight, lil mama. Go enjoy yourself."

"I'm trying to but you're not cooperating." She reached over and grabbed his dick.

Young Milli knocked her hand off of him and eased over, creating space between them. "You trippin', shorty, and Ion get down like that. Now, go enjoy the party." He made sure he put some authority in his voice. He didn't know if it was the liquor, or what, making her come on to him like that, but he wasn't feeling Simona's vibe.

Aria returned from the bathroom to find Milli sitting down and babysitting his drink. "You good? Nothing happened, did it?" Aria thought back to the run-in he had with the opp the other day.

"I'm good, beautiful. Are you enjoying yourself?"

"I am." Young Milli could hear the excitement in her voice and didn't want to ruin her night. Truth be told, he was ready to drop Simona's ass off.

"I'm glad you're enjoying yourself."

"I'll enjoy it even more if you get up and dance with me." Aria grabbed Milli by the arms and pulled him up with his assistance. It didn't take long for him to snap out of his funk and get back to normal.

From across the room, he spotted Simona staring in his direction. Young Milli made it known who he wanted by being frisky with his hands and kissing all over Aria. At one point, he saw Simona roll her eyes. *This bitch is shady,* he thought.

"Let's roll, ma. I'm ready to go," he told Aria.

"Okay."

The first stop they made after they left Escobar's was to drop off Simona. Milli wasn't feeling that creep ass stunt she tried to pull. Aria kicked her shoes off and placed them in his lap. "Can you rub my feet, please? They hurt."

Milli started to massage Aria's feet. "How close are you and your cousin?"

"We're sort of close. I've tried to be like a big sister to her. Our parents are sister and brother. Why do you ask?"

Milli eyed Aria and cleared his throat. "You need to watch out for her. Shorty ain't right." He gave her a rundown of what occurred between them. "I'm not telling you this to cause y'all to fall out or no shit like that. But I don't respect that shady shit she tried. At the very least, you need to know that she'll cross you. Now you know how to deal with her. "

"That lil dirty bitch," Aria seethed. She wanted to turn around so she could beat Simona's ass for disrespecting her and Milli. But she knew that he wouldn't agree to it, so she kept that thought to herself, knowing that Simona had to see her again and it was going to be sooner than later.

Chapter 11

Last night, after coming back from the club, Aria was unusually quiet. Milli knew what he had told her about her cousin was still on her mind. He had no regrets other than it obviously changed Aria's mood. But no matter how bitter it tasted, he believed she was better off knowing that Simona was not to be trusted. They hadn't made love last night but they cuddled, and Aria fell asleep in his arms.

Milli awakened early that Sunday morning with something heavy on his mind, too. Something that he had to deal with every December 19th since he was sixteen years old. It was the anniversary of his mother's passing. Deidre Harris had died from a brain aneurysm at the age of forty years young.

As Milli got dressed to go visit her grave, he smiled at the many memories he had of her. No matter what he'd done, his mother had always been his biggest supporter and staunchest defender. She had always told him that he was destined for stardom, even when he was doing nothing but wilding in the streets and putting his dream of making it in the rap game on the backburner.

Standing in the mirror, shirtless, he touched the image of her face that was tatted on his shoulder. He took a deep breath to stop himself from tearing up. Life was treating him lovely, but he would've given up all the money, cars and fame to bring her back. *Fuck!* She was too good of a woman to earn her angel wings so soon.

He heard Aria stir in bed.

"Bae, what time is it?" She rubbed her eyes.

"It's early, luv. Go back to sleep. I gotta step out for a minute. I'm having this gourmet chef I know come over and cook you breakfast around ten. Damu will be here to let them in."

Aria sat up in bed. She heard something in his voice that worried her. "Is everything okay?" she asked.

"Yes, I'm going to put flowers on my mom's grave."

"I can go with you."

"Nah, I like to do this alone," he said softly, mindful not to hurt her feelings.

"I understand," Aria said. He had told her a lot about his mother so she knew that he was hurting. She got up, walked over to where Milli stood, hugged him from behind and rested her head against his back. No words were necessary, she just wanted to comfort him.

They stood there for a long while, until Milli turned around and kissed her on the forehead. "Thanks. I'ma get dressed." His voice was filled with grief.

When he went into the bathroom to shower, Aria realized her face was wet with tears.

An hour and a half later, Milli stood at his mother's headstone. The gravesite was well-kept and free of any debris. A strong wind whipped around his head. The temperature had dropped significantly overnight but his insulated Burberry bomber jacket protected him from the cold. He had already placed the arrangement of colorful flowers around her plot.

"Good morning, angel," he said as he sat down and placed his back against the large tombstone. His bpv bunched up at his waist, but Young Milli ignored the slight discomfort. "Here I go again." He ran a hand down his face to wipe away the flood of tears that he couldn't contain. "Ma, it's been eleven years but it don't get no easier." He let out a whoosh of breath. "I would give everything I have just for you to be here with me. Even if it was just for one day."

Milli leaned his head against her headstone. Every year that they'd had together ran through his mind in vivid clarity and in slow motion. He laughed at many of the memories and cried at some of the others. He talked to her about his success as well as his troubles. He knew that she was watching down on him, observing his moves without judgment. Because that was her way.

He remembered when she found out that he was in the streets dealing drugs. She told him that he didn't have to do that. *But if that's what you choose to do, you better make muthafuckaz respect you. Don't be a worker, be a boss. Stack your money and don't let nobody take nothing from you. And if you catch a case, you do your time like a man. Because I'm not raising no fuckin' snitch.*

"That was some real shit, Mama," he said now, recalling her advice verbatim. "I'm still in the game but not for much longer. This rap thing has bubbled. Your baby boy lit. But Ion een wanna talm 'bout dat. You know what I wanna talk about, don't you?" He chuckled and a smile replaced his tears. "Ma, I think she might be the one. Straight up. And you know I don't usually talk like this. So, let me know what you think."

Milli closed his eyes and captured the full effect of his mama's spirit. He sat there for almost an hour and soaked up her advice. He could hear his mother's voice in his head and feel it in his soul, as if she was sitting right next to him. She told him everything he needed to hear.

By the time he stood up to leave, he knew without a doubt that Aria was a keeper. He told himself that if he was going to have her in his life for more than a brief period of time, he would have to shield her from the dangers that came with his lifestyle.

From the cemetery, Young Milli drove to meet up with his shoe connect. He had ordered several pair of Red Bottoms for Aria, and a pair of Adidas Women's Yeezy 950 Boot Turtle

Dove Women's Sneakers, along with the latest women's Yeezy's that had dropped a week or so ago. He hoped she would like his selections.

On the way back to the house, K-dog was telling him that one of the young boys that pushed work for them had started hustling on his own since they were told to close down shop. Milli's mouth got tight.

"That's that hot boy shit. Tell that nigga he know the rules. We move in unison."

"He knows that. Niggas just hardheaded and selfish," said K-dog.

Milli nodded his head while quickly deciding the young boy's fate. He realized that youngin's pockets might be leaking, even though the whole squad had always been coached to save money for rainy days. "Find out if he needs some bread. If so, give him fifty racks but tell him to sit his ass down. And that's coming from the top. If he continues to make moves, do what you gotta do."

"Say less."

Milli hoped the youngin wouldn't force his hand. The kid was a good hustla and a certified baby goon. He didn't want to turn the boy's lights out, but he would do it in a heartbeat before he would let him put them all at risk. It didn't take but one slip up to cause a domino effect.

Having addressed the situation, Milli went on Instagram to see what was going on. The first thing he saw was a video of BNK popping off about their encounter at the club the other night. "The next time I see you, bro, it's on and popping. Believe dat! We gon run yo bitch ass off stage at yo own show. Big facts!" BNK said.

Young Milli shook his head. *Real killas don't talk about it. We be about it. Clown ass nigga. Instagram gangsta. You know my get-down.* He was going to put BNK on a t-shirt. *It's on, on sight!* Milli told himself that the next time he ran into that fuck nigga, he was going to pour him out.

For the moment, he pushed that bullshit to the back of his mind and headed home to his Queen. The one he knew his mama thought highly of. He couldn't wait to surprise Aria with the shoes and to see her face light up with that beautiful smile of hers.

***

Aria's thoughts were on Milli. It was her first time seeing him in an emotional state to where he was on the brink of tears. She felt his pain through the energy he displayed. The sadness in his eyes made her want to cry a river, but she managed to hold back her tears to keep from making the situation worse. He wasn't the average street nigga. Milli was a gentle beast with a giving, yet kind heart. That's what made him human.

Aria's thoughts drifted back to last night's events and she couldn't shake the disdain she felt in her heart for Simona. She would've never thought that her cousin would try to sleep with someone she had dealings with.

While they were in the studio, Aria noticed that Simona kept staring at Young Milli with googly eyes and shit. And every time she would dance, she would make sure to do it close enough to where she was in his sight. Her actions should've been seen as red flags, but Aria shrugged it off as Simona being excited about seeing her favorite rapper. Now that she knew that wasn't the case it fueled her rage even further. Simona was on that cousin Faith shit from the movie Soul Food. The only difference was Simona was getting her ass whooped on sight.

At first, Aria was going to keep it to herself, but decided that it was best to let it be known that she was aware of her foul behavior. She was raised to speak her mind at all times whether it hurt their feelings or not. Aria was taught by her mother in her early twenties, that she should live in her truth. She did that daily and today was no different. Snatching up her cellphone, she called Simona.

"Hey, cuz. What's up, girl?" Simona rolled her eyes at the sound of her cousin's voice.

Aria could smell the phoniness seeping through the receiver and it infuriated her. "Cut the bullshit, Simona. I know what happened between you and Milli last night," she spat angrily.

"I don't know what you're talking about," Simona dummied up.

"Oh, he told me what you said and did. That's some foul ass shit you pulled. You that hard up to fuck a nigga in the rap game that you'll cross your family over some dick? Because that's all it would've been. Don't no real man put claims on a bitch that does shit like that."

Simona laughed. "Girl, you need to calm down. It ain't that serious. How long you think you gone last with a nigga like Milli, anyway? He's out of your league. He needs a young bitch on his arm, not a big sister."

"Out of my league?" Aria snapped. "Hoe, you are out of *your* league. My nigga don't want no washed up, ran through ho' on his arm. So, you better watch that mouth that's used as a cum bucket before I wire that shit shut."

"Oh, you slut shaming now? That's just like sadity ass Aria to turn her nose down on kinfolk just because she graduated college and bought a lil house. Girl, bye, you ain't no better than me."

"And is! You jealous ass hoe. Whose fault is it that you spent the last eight years in Georgia and still don't have a fuckin' degree. If you spent more time in the classroom instead of on your back and knees at the trap house you'll be on my level."

"Fuck you! Niggas like Milli want a yellow bone, not a brown-skinned fake-ass Barbie. I can't wait for that nigga to break your heart for a young bitch like me. Maybe that'll knock your boujee ass of those fluffy clouds your high and mighty ass been sitting on. Then you can use those same clouds to wipe your tears."

Aria had enough of slick rappin' with Simona. She was trying to hit below the belt. It was time to break that bitch down and close her mouth for good. "I should've seen this shit coming a mile away from a crack baby."

Simona cut her off. "Bitch, I ain't no crack baby."

"Bitch, ask your daddy, my uncle, where you really come from. His wife can't have kids. Your real mother was a crackhead and my uncle was her drug dealer. She sold you for an eight-ball and a hundred dollars. And when I catch you, I'm beating your ass, so you better keep that nappy ass head and wig on a swivel, hoe."

"Fuck you, lying ass bitch." Simona's voice cracked right along with her heart. Her eyelids were now coated with tears. Aria hit her with a possible truth that had never been revealed during a messy family dinner. For years, she wondered why she didn't look like either of her parents. Simona was high-yellow, but her parents were darker than her. If what she'd heard was the God's honest truth, that meant that Simona's entire life was built on lies.

The call ended abruptly.

Aria's phone slipped from her fingertips and hit the floor. A heavy stream of tears cascaded down her smooth, brown skin. It was never her intention to reveal the family's secret, but Simona pushed buttons that couldn't stop her wrath.

The sound of the door closing, shook Aria from her past. She could hear Young Milli's footsteps down the hall. She jumped up and ran into the bathroom. He had enough going on and didn't need to be wrapped up in her family drama. Aria turned on the faucet, so that she could wash away her tears. Just as she was drying her face, Milli walked in with a smile on his face.

"Good morning, beautiful." He wrapped his arms around her waist and kissed her forehead. "It's time for breakfast."

"Okay," she nodded. "Give me a few minutes and I'll be right down."

"A'ight."

Young Milli walked away leaving Aria alone. She needed a few minutes to get her thoughts together and push that negative energy to the side. She was not about to allow thoughts of Simona ruin her breakfast date with her king.

Aria walked downstairs to the large kitchen area dressed in a bright pink Versace robe with the matching slippers. The chef greeted her with a smile. "Good morning, Ms. Aria. He's out back waiting on you."

"Good morning and thank you." She eyed the small fruit platter. "May I help myself to these?"

"Absolutely."

"Thanks," she replied sweetly.

Aria grabbed the tray and made her way through the double glass doors that led to the backyard while smacking on a juicy strawberry. Milli was seated at a patio table decorated for two. The Olympic sized pool sparkled against the sun. It was quiet and peaceful. Soft sounds of the waterfall were the only thing that could be heard.

"Wow, I didn't know you had a lake behind your house. It's beautiful back here."

"Thanks."

"If I would've known it was like that back here, I would've come out earlier to get my thoughts together." Aria walked past Milli, but he grabbed ahold of her robe.

"Give me one of those strawberries."

She picked up one from the tray and placed it in between her teeth. "Here." Milli grabbed the strawberry from her mouth and pecked her lips during the process.

Within a few minutes, the chef delivered their food on a silver platter. "Enjoy."

They feasted on waffles, grits, eggs, steak, and soft buttermilk biscuits. The only sound that could be heard were their forks. Aria used the orange juice and wine to make two Mimosas. He was skeptical at first, but he decided to partake in the mixed concoction she created.

Milli sat his fork down and wiped his mouth with a cloth napkin. His eyes were trained on Aria. "You wanna tell me what was on your mind earlier? You seemed bothered."

"It was nothing," she lied. The truth was it was Simona's action that stirred constantly in her mind.

"I won't press you, but if you want to talk about it, let me know."

Aria's eyes said okay, but her lips said nothing.

"I'll be right back."

Within minutes, Aria's cellphone vibrated in her pocket. When she pulled it out, her stomach turned at the sight of Jaheim calling. Her first mind said ignore it, but her gut said answer it. "What do you want?"

"Why haven't you called me?"

"Because I don't need to. We're not together anymore, so stop calling me."

"Is it because you up there with that nigga Young Milli? And don't lie. Your cousin told me and I saw the pictures and videos on that nigga's IG page."

"That's not any of your business because I don't owe you an explanation."

"Oh, you owe me one. How the fuck you think that makes me look. My woman in another state being a groupie chick to a rap dude. Did you fuck that nigga?"

Aria was heated at the fact Simona was telling her business to Jaheim. "If I did fuck him, that's my business."

"Aria, did you fuck this man and don't lie to me?"

"Is that what you want to know?" Aria was sick of Jaheim and the drama that came along with him. Adding fuel to the fire, she laughed at him and gave him an earful in hopes that he would leave her alone. "As a matter of fact, I did, several times at that. I sucked his dick, too." Her aim was to damage his ego. It worked because Jaheim's blood was boiling like hot grits.

"So, you up there being a hoe? You know that's what he thinks of you right? You so fuckin' stupid. Wait until I see you. Your ass gone pay for this. Mark my fuckin' words."

"It's funny you say that. I've been stupid for you for two years, but I guess that was fine. Say what you want, but the fact of the matter is this *man* has treated me better in three days than you've done in twenty-four months."

From a distance, she could see Milli heading towards the door. "I have to go. My man is here and don't call my phone because I'm blocking you. Now, have a nice life with your broke ass baby mama and leave me the fuck alone." Aria hung up in his face and put him on the block list right along with *scam likely.*

Chapter 12

"Problems?" Milli asked in a non-accusatory tone. He had caught the tail end of her conversation.

"No, I don't have any problems, bae. That was the ex calling me on some dumb stuff. But he's blocked now."

"You should've been done that," he said.

"You're right, and I apologize for not having done it before now," Aria owned her mistake. "But trust and believe I don't have a reason to talk to him. It's all about you."

Milli sat the shoe boxes down that he was carrying. He shoved his hands down inside his pants pockets and stared into Aria's eye. "Luv, let me ask you something. And I want you to keep it a stack. Ya feel me?"

"Yes. You can ask me anything, Milli. And you don't have to remind me to keep it real. I'll never do anything but that," she vowed.

"Cool. Well, answer this: I know you and dude have history, and sometimes that's hard to walk away from. Are you conflicted?"

Aria looked Milli dead in the eye. "Baby, there's not a conflicted vessel in my heart. I know who I want, unequivocally. And that's you."

"You sure about that?"

"Did I stutter?"

"I'm just saying, luv. Because if you are…"

"The question has been asked and answered!" He was starting to make her ass itch with that nonsense. "I don't want Jaheim. That ship has passed. If I wasn't all into you and only you, I wouldn't be here, Milli. I'm not that type of woman. I would never lay in your arms while my mind is on some other nigga. If you think that little of me, you can take me to the airport. Or I'll call an Uber." Tears of anger welled up in her eyes.

"Whoa! C'mere, luv." Young Milli pulled her into his arms and kissed away her tears. "It's nothing like that. I was just offering you an out if you were having a change of heart."

"Let me go!" Aria tried to shove him away but he was too strong.

"What's wrong with you?" Milli chuckled then licked his sexy ass lips. Aria both hated and loved the fact that he could stir her emotions so soon.

"Did I ask for an out, sir?"

"Oh, it's *sir* now? Watch me make you change that shit back to bae."

Milli untied her robe, and covered her left breast with his mouth as his fingers found her center. Aria was already wet. He hoisted her up, so that her legs were on his shoulders, and walked her back against the glass doors. Aria's pussy pressed against his mouth. He used his tongue to softly lick her folds.

"Oh, my gawd!" Aria held on to his dreads.

Milli found her swollen clit and began to trace the ABC's on it. By the time he got to the letter T, Aria rewarded him with her sweet nectar.

She could barely stand when he placed her feet on the ground. "You know you're about to get punished for calling me sir, don't you?" Milli made her face the wall. He lifted the bottom of her robe up, exposing all ass.

"Punish me, daddy," Aria cried in anticipation.

"Oh, it's daddy now? What happened to *sir*?"

"It's always been daddy from the moment you first touched me."

Milli was rock muhfuckin' hard. That dick felt like a steel beam going inside Aria's heated pussy. He slammed in and out of her forcefully and with purpose. Her juices coated his rod and put a battery in his back. He was geeked.

"Who's ya nigga, huh?"

"Deontay Harris!" She called out his government name.

"Who?" Milli drew back to the tip then went back in, balls deep.

"Young Milli!" Aria screamed in ecstasy.

"You mine, ain't you? Ain't you?" He pounded her into submission.

"Yes, daddy. I'm yours. All yours!" Aria moaned as they came together.

Aria was so weak, Milli had to half-carry her up to the bedroom. He allowed her a few minutes to recuperate then he went to retrieve her gifts.

"For my Queen," he said, presenting the shoe boxes to her.

"You're the best," she beamed, as she opened them one by one and squealed with delight at each pair.

"You know you got a nigga hooked, right?" Milli said, taking her hand into his.

"Correction." Aria put up the other hand like a stop sign. "You got *me* hooked. I have never felt for any man what I feel for you. And it happened this quick." She snapped her fingers.

"That's 'cause it's real. Our chemistry is one thousand," he exclaimed.

"Yes, bae, it is." Aria had to agree with that.

"Now, tell me, what would you like to do today?"

"We could stay in bed all day and you could punish me some more." Aria put her finger in her mouth and looked at him impishly.

"Shorty, you ain't about that life."

"I'm really not," she laughed. "You be putting it on my ass. Messing with you I'm going to end up in traction."

They joked around for a few minutes then went to bathe together. Milli promised to be good, but ten minutes after getting in the bathtub, his dick kept jumping out of the water. Aria wasn't built for round two, not that morning.

"I'm not messing with you," she said, hurrying out of the tub and getting in the shower.

"Scary ass," Milli laughed.

Chapter 13

The Wednesday before Christmas rolled around and found Aria stretched out across the bed watching Milli get dressed. She covered her mouth while releasing a big yawn. "Where are you going?"

"I have some important business to handle. I'll be back in a few hours."

Aria thought long and hard for a few seconds. She had been waiting for the moment that Milli left her alone. She had something to handle, too, and today was a good day to take care of it. "Well, I'm going to go to the mall while you're out." She tossed the covers back and climbed out of bed.

"I'll have Damu take you," he insisted.

"No. I'm good. I can take an Uber."

"Nah!" Milli buckled his belt and cut his eyes in Aria's direction. "I'm not letting you go out by yourself. You can take the driver or wait until I get back. The choice is yours." Milli laid down the law and waited on her to respond.

"Fine," she pouted and walked away. "I'll take the driver." She was not happy with his response, but she was unwilling to start an unnecessary fight over it.

Milli grinned at her stubbornness. "I thought you would see it my way. Now, come back and kiss your king before he leaves."

Aria spun around full-circle and headed in his direction with a slight attitude. Their eyes were locked and so were their lips for a brief moment.

"See you later."

"I see I have to break you out of that stubborn shit and soon." Milli grabbed his strap and walked out of the room.

Aria wasn't happy that she was stuck with Damu for the day. It wasn't because she didn't like him, but the simple fact that she had something planned and didn't need him reporting back to Milli. He didn't do drama, so she knew it would be a problem. But she would cross that bridge when she got to it.

After handling all of her morning ablutions, Aria dressed in tomboy gear— jeans, pullover sweater and a pair of Air Force 1's. She tied her hair up in a simple ponytail and lotioned her face. Damu drove her to Lennox Mall in Milli's G-wagon. The ride was silent for the most part, but Aria was curious about something that he could help with. "Damu, I have a question for you."

"What's that?" His eyes never left the road.

"What do you buy a man that has everything? I've been debating with myself for days about what I should get him for Christmas and I'm stuck. I've never been in this position before."

"Believe it or not Milli easy to please. Although bro is flashy and all that, he appreciates the small things in life. Whatever you get him, I'm sure he will treasure it. Simply because it came from you."

Aria sighed and folded her arms across her chest in frustration. "I need some direction. I'm stuck. I know it's the thought that counts, but I want to make him happy on Christmas day."

"All I can say is give from the heart. He would appreciate that more than the gift itself." Damu took his eyes off of the road for a millisecond. "On a serious note, between me and you, my dude likes you a lot. I knew that when he brought you to his house. He's never done that before. So, stay real with him and take care of his heart."

Aria could sense the seriousness in his firm tone. Therefore, she agreed. "I will," she promised.

For an hour or more, Aria and Damu walked the mall without a gift in hand. When they passed a jewelry store for the second time, Aria stopped and pointed towards the entrance. "Let's go in here. I think I know the perfect gift for him."

When they went into the store, Aria spotted exactly what she had in mind. During the two hours, it would take for the jeweler to customize the order, they sat down inside of Cajun Supreme for a bite to eat. She was in the mood for Chinese that day.

After lunch, they stopped at a few stores where she bought a couple of designer outfits for Milli, several pairs of shoes and a massage table. Now she was glad to have Damu with her. Not only did she feel protected, but she had someone to carry her bags. By the time they made their way back to the jeweler, Aria's gifts were ready. The design of the custom piece was stunning and it had come from the heart. She knew that Milli would love it. She couldn't wait to see the smile on his face when she gave him his presents.

"Where to now?" asked Damu on their way to the vehicle.

Aria checked her watch. The timing was perfect for her to execute this final part of her plan.

"Can you take me by my cousin's. I want to drop off something I owe her." It wasn't really a lie.

"No problem." Damu didn't give it a second thought.

When they pulled up to Simona's apartment, her car wasn't there. Aria checked the time in her phone. It was 4:15. If she recalled correctly, Simona came home from work around 4:30. "I'm sorry she won't be home for another fifteen minutes," she apologized to Damu.

"Ain't no pressure," he assured her.

While they waited, Aria tightened her shoe laces and covered her face in baseline lip balm. *Just in case the bitch tries to scratch me.* She didn't have to wait long before Simona drove up in her Kia Soul, oblivious to what she was coming home to. Aria saw that Simona's roommate, Gina, was in the passenger seat. In her present state of mind, Aria didn't care. Gina could get it, too. *Bitch would be wise to mind her own business, though.*

As soon as the girls parked and got out of the car, Aria made her move. Simona was preoccupied with her phone, so she didn't realize what was popping off until Aria's fist slammed into her face. Simona stumbled and her phone hit the ground.

Whack! Whack! Aria hit her with a two-piece that knocked her on her ass. "Bitch, didn't I tell you it was on sight when I caught you." Aria stood over her, glaring down.

Simona scooted back and then pounced to her feet with the quickness of a feline. "Oh, you gotta sneak a bitch? I'm 'bout to kick your ass, ho" Simona attacked, swinging wildly with both fists. She landed a blow on the top of Aria's head, but the others missed.

Aria shook that shit off and bopped her in the mouth with a left-right combination that knocked Simona into a neighbor's car. The alarm blared loudly, but that didn't stop Aria. She reached out, grabbed Simona by her long wig, wrapped it around her hand, and jerked her cousin's head down. "Talk slick now, bitch!" Uppercut after uppercut landed squarely on Simona's mouth.

"Bitch, let my hair go," she shouted out of breath and swinging her arms like a windmill.

"I told you I was gone beat your ass for trying me. It ain't even about Milli at this point 'cause he wouldn't fuck you with another nigga's dick."

"Let go of my fuckin' hair!"

"This ain't your hair, bald headed thot. You bought it." *Whack! Whack! Whack!*

Gina looked on, unsure if she should help Simona or not. She was a straight up hood chick, who knew that people were killed jumping in other people's beefs. Besides, she knew Simona and Aria were family, and that Simona had did some real hoe shit. *She deserves this ass whooping,* Gina concluded.

Aria continued to rain blows on Simona's face until she felt Damu step in and grab her hands. "Let her go." Then he looked over at Gina, "Grab ya friend," he yelled. As they pulled them in opposite directions, Aria kicked Simona in the stomach.

It took a few minutes, but Damu was finally able to get them separated. Aria was holding Simona's wig in her hand and twirling it in the air. "You want this back, you baldheaded ass hoe?" she teased.

Simona, bloody mouth and all, tried to run towards Aria, but Gina held her back. "Bitch, this shit ain't over. Watch what I tell you," Simona hurled. Her face was bruised and her lip was busted. "I'ma hit you where it hurts, so be ready."

Damu held onto Aria so that she couldn't get away from him and escorted her back to the car. "You mad 'cause I beat that ass," she screamed. "Go fuck for a new wig, hoe. Cause you ain't getting this one back."

Damu put Aria inside of the car and got in on the driver's side. "That was your cousin from the other night?" he asked.

"Yeah."

"You know Milli gone be mad when he finds out about this, right? You shouldn't be out here scrapping with your cousin like that. But you know I gotta tell him. I keep it G wit' the homie." Damu let it be known.

"As you should. And if he gets mad at me, I'll wear that. Because I owed that bitch that ass kicking, cousin or not." Aria folded her arms across her chest and stared out of the passenger window.

The ride was silent on the way back to the house. Aria hoped that Milli wasn't there just yet. She needed to calm down and have a drink before discussing what happened. But when they arrived, he was home.

***

To Aria's surprise, Milli didn't fuss at her.

"I understand why you did what you did, but that's it. Let it go. I don't want you out here squabbling with nobody. You're too pretty and classy for that shit," he said, sitting beside her on the living room sofa.

"Humph."

"What that mean, champ?" he laughed.

"You know." Aria tried not to crack a smile.

"Fa real, luv. You can't go around beating up every female that throws herself at me. That's gon' happen. The thirst is real."

"I know that but—"

"It's different because she's your cousin, and family should never cross family, right?"

"That part."

"I get it. And that's why I'm not tripping. But that's it. It's over. I'm not asking you, I'm telling you." He left no room for debate.

"Okay, bae. It's over with," Aria promised.

Little did she know, Simona wanted revenge in the worst way.

Chapter 14

"This bitch got me all the way fucked up," Simona yelled as she stood in the bathroom cleaning the dried blood from her lip.

Gina was sitting on the bed listening to her rant and rave about the fight. "Why you so hyped up? You was dead-ass wrong for doing that to your cousin."

"Fuck her! That ain't her nigga no way." She continued to spazz out. "She's known this nigga for a few days and all of a sudden they're a couple. Chyy bye!"

"It doesn't matter. She's with him and that means he's off limits to you. Duh!" Gina shook her head.

Simona stopped patting her lip with the cotton ball soaked in peroxide and faced Gina. "Well, damn, bitch, who side you on? You're my friend, not hers."

"This ain't about sides. It's about right and wrong, and friend, you were wrong. And I would be less of a friend if I didn't tell you the truth." Gina laid across the bed with her chin propped against her knuckles. "That's that weird shit and if one of my cousins did that to me, I would beat her ass, too."

"Girl, what you mean by, too? Aria did not whoop my ass."

"Umm. She really did, sis. I saw the fight."

"The bitch stole me. And she grabbed my hair. If she hadn't did that, I would've dragged that hoe."

"I's cool. You can't win them all."

"Whatever!" Simona walked out of the bathroom to retrieve her phone from the dresser. "I might've lost the fight, but I'm about to win this battle. Just wait and see." She flopped down on the bed and opened up her Instagram.

"What are you about to do?"

"You'll see."

The phone rang numerous times before someone picked up. "Yo!"

"What you doing?"

"Chillin'. What's good?" Jaheim stepped out of the bedroom to keep from awakening his son and to keep Mya out of his business.

"I think you should come up here for Christmas. That's the only way you gone get Aria back."

"Ion believe that."

"I'm telling you the truth. We was drinking and she told me what she said to you. The girl was over here crying because she wants to take you back. She was only with Milli to make you jealous." Simona laid that lie on nice and thick.

"No, bullshit?"

"No, bullshit. I am her cousin so I would know. Catch you a flight here and get your girl back. Young Milli will be performing at Club Onyx on Christmas Eve. That will be the perfect time for y'all to talk."

"I'll see if I can find a flight."

"Nigga, make that shit happen," Simona sighed heavily into the receiver. "Listen to me, you need to make sure you get here by Friday. If you want her back, a plane ticket shouldn't be standing in your way. That nigga surprised her and flew her up here. She likes shit like that. Do you really think she'll turn you down if you flew to another state to beg for her forgiveness? That shit is romantic as fuck, so get here. And you can stay here at the house with me and my roommate."

"A'ight. I'm about to look for a flight now." Jaheim could feel someone's presence in the room. When he looked up, Mya was standing by the sofa with her hands on her hips giving him a death stare. "What? Why you being so goddamn nosey?" he snapped.

"I know damn well you not about to leave me and your son here during the holidays. Where are you catching a flight to, Jaheim? I know damn well you better not be planning nothing with Aria." Mya was furious.

"Chill the fuck out. That might not be my baby anyway." Jaheim wanted her to get the fuck away from him and fast. "Go back in the room and I'm not saying it again." Mya stomped off huffing, puffing, and cursing him out.

"I see you have problems all across the board. You need to get your bitches in line and get a slight getaway," Simona giggled.

"I'll message you when I find a flight."

"Okay."

Simona ended the call and looked up to find Gina eyeballing her. "You refuse to learn your lesson. Why you got that man coming here? That's just messy as hell."

"Girl, I do not care about none of that."

"Okay. When she beat your ass again, I'm not breaking up shit."

"Just get out of my room, thank you."

"No worries, boo. I've been put out of better places by better people." Gina chucked up the peace sign on her way out.

"You ain't never been put out by a bad bitch like me," Simona hissed and fell back onto the bed with a devious smile on her face. She couldn't wait to see the look on Aria's face when she saw Jaheim.

***

Jaheim went on Young Milli's IG page to confirm what Simona told him. He saw that the nigga was performing exactly where she said he would be on Christmas Eve. He also found himself looking at the videos of Young Milli and Aria at the club again. He had seen them before, but that didn't lessen the bitterness he felt, seeing her hugged up with a nigga who looked to be fresh out of high school. *Why is she acting like a got dam cougar?*

Scrolling further down Young Milli's page, Jaheim saw the many pictures of him balling: the cars, jewels, money and gear. He didn't believe that none of that shit really belonged to Young Milli. Many rappers faked it for the gram and other social media sites. *That nigga ain't got that type of dough.* Jaheim refused to believe that Young Milli had that type of bank.

Jealousy invaded his heart like a malignant disease. Filled with envy, he logged off of Instagram and went on Facebook to scour Aria's page. What he saw enraged him. One post after the other spoke of a new found love that made her happier than she'd ever been in her life. She hadn't mentioned that young boy by name, but Jaheim knew who the fuck she was referring to. He couldn't recall the last time Aria had declared her affection for him on her page. Jaheim felt played. Yeah, he had fucked up, but if she thought Young Milli was gonna be faithful, she was gonna be in for a rude awakening, Jaheim fumed.

But if Aria was so happy, why did she tell Simona that she wanted to get back with him, he wondered. *She was only with Milli to make you jealous.*

"Why would Simona lie about that?" he said out loud.

Since he couldn't come up with a logical answer, Jaheim accepted it as the truth. Either way, it was time for him to reclaim his girl. Fuck letting her run around snapping pictures on the next nigga's arm. She was making him look like a clown to anyone that knew they used to be together. Fuck that, he was J-A-H-E-I-M! Women didn't leave him, he kicked *them* to the curb.

I'ma get her back. And when I do, I'ma dog her ass out. And if that young boy got a problem with me coming up there to reclaim my bitch, I'ma show him that it's real out here in these streets. I know niggas that'll take his head off.

Jaheim's mind was made up. He was going to Atlanta to get what was his. Aria was coming back to him by choice or force.

Chapter 15

"You wanna get in the Jacuzzi?" Milli asked Aria.

"And do what? Freeze to death? No, thank you, sir," Aria tried to keep a straight face since he hated to be called sir.

He stopped scrolling through his phone and cut his eyes in Aria's direction. "We back on that sir shit again? Do I need to remind you what my name is?"

She thought back to the pleasurable punishment he laid down on the patio and felt little bolts shoot through her vajayjay. "No, sir!" she giggled. "You are bae aka daddy."

"That's what I thought." Milli sat his phone down on the bed. His attention was elsewhere. "We getting in the Jacuzzi or nah?"

"Bae, is it cold, or not?"

"It's not. The sun is out. We'll be fine." Milli grabbed Aria by the arm and pulled her on top of him. "Besides, the Casamigos and sexual energy between us will keep us warm." He placed his hand on the nape of her neck and kissed her. Aria felt strong, erotic chills down her spine.

"You right about that. Let's do it."

The warm sunrays beamed on the back of Aria's neck as she removed the robe she was wearing and dropped it on the lawn chair. Milli snapped a few pictures of her sexiness in the two-piece bikini that she wore so well.

"You and that phone of yours," she smiled

"Just capturing the beautiful parts of my life." Milli smiled back at her.

It wasn't cold outside, but it wasn't hot either. Rapid bubbles circulated in the tub. Aria stuck her big toe in the water to test the warmth of it. It was to her satisfaction, so she stepped inside, lowered her body into the heated water and made her way to where Milli was relaxing.

"You couldn't take my word for it, huh?" Milli chuckled. "This ain't the blind leading the blind."

"I had to be sure you weren't trying to trick me."

"I'll never do that." Milli grabbed a freshly poured glass of Casamigos and handed it to Aria. "We turning up indoors today since I'll be performing tomorrow night at Onyx."

"That sounds like a plan," Aria agreed. It didn't matter if they went out or stayed locked in. As long as she was in his company that was all that mattered.

"Speaking of which, I need to post a promo video for my fans. We need a packed house on Christmas Eve." Milli grabbed his phone that rested on the concrete and opened his Instagram. As soon as he logged in, he had thirty thousand viewers on his live and they were commenting like crazy. "Yo, this your boy Young Milli and I just wanna remind y'all to pull up at club Onyx tomorrow night. Your boy will be in the building performing live. And if you miss me on Christmas Eve, you can catch me at Diamond's the day after Christmas. I'll be ripping shit all holiday season, rolling into 2022. Be there. It's gon' me lit."

Young Milli verbally responded to his homies' comments and only a few of the fans. He looked at Aria and smiled, "They wanna know who is the female that's been in my lives and photos lately."

"Who am I?" Aria blushed hard enough for her cheekbones to sit high and damn near close her eyes when he turned the camera towards her face. She wasn't expecting to be put on the spot like that.

"This is bae. Damn right," he responded to one of his followers, and then he pulled Aria close, kissing her on live.

102

More comments poured in. "They said you're pretty," he relayed.

"Thank you."

"Alright, y'all. Me and bae signing off so we can enjoy this Jacuzzi. And don't forget club Onyx tomorrow night. Diamond's the day after Christmas. Love." He ended the live and placed his focus back on Aria.

One hour in and two drinks later, Aria was truly feeling the heat on her body and between her thighs. She couldn't keep her hands and mouth off of Milli. He closed his eyes when he felt her hand grip his limp pole and suck on his neck. "Can you make it get it up underwater?"

"What do you mean?" she asked.

"Can you hold your breath under water?" His question was more precise.

Aria moved her head so that she could look him in the eyes. "I surely can. I'm a good swimmer."

"Let me see," he replied with a sly grin on his face.

"Nah, boo. That sounds like a deadly task. Now, what you can do is sit on that step and let me do my thang."

"Say less." Milli switched places, rested his elbows on the concrete, and closed his eyes, while Aria went to work.

***

While Aria was satisfying her new man, her ex woke up on a mission that morning. His bag was already packed and sitting by the front door. He started off with a shot of Tito's and a hot shower. Mya was sitting on the bed with her arms folded and a mean mug on her face.

"So, you really about to leave us here on Christmas?"

"We already discussed this." He walked past her and started to get dressed. "So, don't start that shit. It's too early in the morning to be arguing."

"But this is our first Christmas as a family," she whined. "We are supposed to spend it together."

"The baby is two months. He don't understand shit about Christmas. I'll be back in a few days and that's final."

"Yeah, a'ight." Mya rolled her eyes and left the room.

It took less than an hour for Jaheim to leave the house and pick up his homeboy, Twan, a young certified killa who was accompanying him on the trip just in case some real drama popped off. Twan threw his bag in the back and hopped into the passenger seat. "What's good, Unc?"

"Shit cooling. Just ready to pull up on this bitch and get some understanding? She got me looking real lame out here."

"I feel you," he nodded. "These bitches think it's a game out here, but they can get it, too. Just like a nigga can. You can't ever let them forget that or they'll have your ass wearing a dress."

Jaheim cut his eyes at Twan. Something warned him not to take his trigger-happy ass with him. He knew the youngsta was about his business, but he was going to be hard to control if things didn't go as planned. Twan had a bad rep in the hood for being thirsty and wanting to call the shots.

"Don't forget, while we're up there you're following my lead. Just watch my back. That's all you gotta do," said Jaheim.

"Unc, how many times are you him gonna tell me that? You already told me that a dozen room times yesterday."

"I'm just making sure it's understood before we pull off."

"I got you, Unc," said Twan, but he was already thinking of a way to flip the situation into more money for himself than

Jaheim was paying him. His pockets were hurting and he needed a quick fix to that problem.

After they left Twan's house, Jaheim slid by the weed man and liquor plug, to get some shit to keep him focused on the road. From there, he filled up the gas tank and jumped onto I-95 North.

"Yo, use my phone and put some tunes on," Jaheim said to Twan.

Through the speakers, Moneybagg Yo played and it was a vibe. Jaheim lit a Black & Mild, cracked the window, and nodded his head to the beat.

A half hour into the ride Young Milli's newest song started to play, changing Jaheim's mood altogether.

"Bruh, can you change that shit?"

"For what, the nigga snapping on the track."

"That nigga is garbage. I don't wanna listen to that lame ass shit," Jaheim barked.

"Unc, I ain't ya bitch. Lower your tone. We both put our pants on the same way." Twan shook his head. He didn't understand why Jaheim was hating on Young Milli. They didn't know each other. In Twan's opinion, his big homie should've let that shit go. *Fuck beefing over a bitch. If this nigga wasn't paying me to roll with him, I wouldn't be down with it.*

"Man, just change the station."

Twan changed the song once he saw how angry it made Jaheim. He went on Milli's Instagram page. "Damn," he shook his head.

"What?" Jaheim turned his head to see what Twan was looking at.

"Unc, keep your eyes on the road."

"Man, I got this. What the hell you looking at, anyway?" Jaheim's curiosity was getting the best of him.

Twan turned the phone so that he could see the screen. All of the blood rushed from Jaheim's face the second he saw Aria on Young Milli's page scantily dressed in a bikini. His hands gripped the steering wheel tightly and a strong vein popped up on his forehead.

"See, this that fuck shit I'm talm 'bout. This bitch steady trying me for the public. I'ma snap her neck in two when I get my hands on her. On God."

"You know that nigga not going to let you get that close to her."

"That's why you're with me," Jaheim reminded him. "If he gets in the way, you deal with him. You brought your heat with you, didn't you?"

"You already know. A nigga like me keep that hammer on him at all times." Twan opened his jacket to expose the butt of the gun that was tucked in his waist. Jaheim nodded his head in approval. He had chosen to drive instead of catching a flight for that exact reason. His lil shotta couldn't have brought his burner on an airplane.

"Don't get trigger happy, though. *Just watch my back.* We ain't going up there to catch a murder case. I'm just going to get my girl back from dude. Hopefully, when I see her, she'll get her mind right."

"And if she don't?"

"She will." Jaheim felt certain of that. He truly believed Aria was doing all of that just to pay him back for having an outside baby with Mya. What he didn't realize was that Aria had gotten a taste of how a real nigga treated a Queen. Jaheim didn't stand a snowball's chance in Hell of ever getting her back. *Periodt!*

Chapter 16

The drive to Atlanta was uneventful. Once they reached the city, Jaheim used his GPS to find Simona's apartment. She opened the door and greeted him like a long lost friend.

"Heyyyy, it's so good to see you." She hugged Jaheim's neck.

He felt a little strange because they had never been that close. "Good to see you, too. This my dawg. Twan. Twan, this Simona." He introduced the two.

A few minutes later, the three of them were passing blunts around and chopping it up. Gina came home a while later and joined in the smokefest. When the liquor came out, Jaheim drank and drank until he became unbelievably angry. He wanted to search every club in Atlanta until he found Aria and Young Milli.

"Do it." Simona gassed him up.

"Nooo! He can't run up on her like that. I don't know what hole y'all been living in, but Young Milli ain't no ho'. You better Google him. He's not just going to let you do that," Gina intoned. She also knew that Simona was using Jaheim to help her get revenge for Aria kicking her ass.

"Bitch, stay out of my business," said Simona in a playful tone, but she was dead serious.

Twan just sat there watching and listening. He had never seen Jaheim so caught up in his feelings and reckless.

Gina got up and went in her room. She had heard enough. She knew Simona could be grimey, but this was taking it to a new level. She was going to mess around and get somebody killed.

Earlier that day, Gina had told a male cousin of hers what Simona was up to.

"Tell your girl not to play with Young Milli like that. Bro ain't to be fucked with. He's about that life fa real, fa real. And he roll with killaz," her cousin had warned.

Gina had tried to convey that to Simona's messy ass, but the trick was too intent on getting her getback on Aria to listen. And Jaheim was pitiful. What type of street nigga let a young, dumb, and full of cum female like Simona trick him into a confrontation that he was likely to lose.

Why is it so hard for niggas to take a L and keep it moving, she wondered. *If Jaheim was that in love with Aria, he wouldn't have cheated on her in the first place. Now he's going through all of this to get a woman back that he should've appreciated when he had her.*

"Niggas don't want you and don't want nobody else to have you," Gina said to the ceiling before turning off her bedside lamp and falling asleep with her clothes on.

When Gina woke up in the middle of the night, everybody was gone. Even Simona.

The next day, Christmas Eve, she found out that they hadn't went looking for Aria and Young Milli, after all.

"We ended up going to Magic City. "Girl, I got fucked up. I popped a Xan and started stripping up in that bitch. Niggas were throwing money and hooting and hollering. I think I found my calling," Simona laughed.

"Bitch, you're ratchet as fuck." Gina started laughing, too. When Simona finished giving her a replay of her stripper debut, she asked where Jaheim and Twan were.

"They got a room," said Simona. "But it's going down tonight. Young Milli is performing at the Onyx and I know Aria will be there. I can't wait to see that ho's face when she sees Jaheim. I'm going *live* with that shit. Put her uppity ass on blast for the whole world to see. Then, Young Milli is going to ghost that bitch."

Simona was certain that her plan would bear fruit.

***

Ghosting, Aria was as far from Young Milli's thoughts as heaven is for a gangsta. Their day had been filled with nothing but budding love, carnal passion, and plenty of laughter and good fun.

On TikTok, Aria had accepted her bestie Brandy's "Can We Talk" challenge. That was the craze of the moment on social media. Her rendition of Tevin Campbell's R&B hit song suprised the hell out of Young Milli, who was right next to her. He hadn't known that his boo had such a beautiful voice.

In the middle of Aria's soulful singing, Young Milli cut in with a freestyle verse that was lethal. The video had gone viral and had gotten over 500,000 views. People wanted to know if Aria was a signed artist. Aria loved the praise, but she didn't take it too serious.

"I gotta get you in the studio. With that voice you can be a star," said Milli.

"No no no!" Aria wagged her finger. She wanted no parts of the limelight. She had grown up singing in the church choir, but that's as far as she'd ever taken it, and she had no plans to change that now. Even her growing love for Milli couldn't convince her to do otherwise.

"A'ight luv," he'd relented.

Night fell and it was time for Aria and Milli to head out to club Onyx. Upon their arrival, the parking lot was packed and the line was damn near wrapped around the building. Everybody and their mammy wanted to come out and party with Young Milli.

Damu opened the backdoor to the limo and stepped to the side. Milli held onto Aria's hand as she stepped out looking like a bag of money in her diamond encrusted body con fitted dress and six inch heels. Her perky breast sat up just right. Milli was rocking urban gear, accentuated by ice that cost more than most rappers' net worth. He could hear a throng of ladies making cat calls and shouting their *I love you's*. He waved to his fans and admirers and kept it pushing towards the security checkpoint.

The club promoter blocked off a private area for Milli and his thirty person entourage. Security was heavy that night, but he already had his goons on deck in case some shit popped off. He could never be too careful. Once seated the bottle girl, who was dressed in a fishnet bodysuit, exposing her pierced nipples, arrived with several bottles. Milli handed her a stack of bills.

"Aye, shorty. Bring me back some ones and you keep five hundred."

Her eyes beamed as bright as the strobe lights when she thumbed through the bills. "Is there anything else that I can get for you?" she asked flirtatiously, as if Aria wasn't sitting directly beside him.

"Nah. That's it."

"Okay, I'll be right back," she smiled and strutted away with an extra swish in her hips.

Aria scanned through the crowd of half-naked women. Only a couple had natural bodies, while the majority of them had overly inflated asses and snatched waistlines. It was easy for her to decipher between the two. But she had to give the girls credit, they were sexy enough to tempt God.

Milli placed his hand on her thigh. "You want a lap dance?"

"No. I'm good."

"Nah, bae. You gotta turn up with me. It's Christmas Eve," he insisted. "I wanna see you get loose."

Aria hesitated. Although, she wasn't into girls, she'd had a lap dance once before. Her reluctance now was because she didn't want Milli getting no ideas about a ménage à trois. That was so *not* going to happen. *But he would never ask me to do that,* she realized.

"Okay. I'll get one," Aria agreed.

"A'ight. Pick a girl."

"I don't know who to pick." That was a little white lie because she had an idea of who she wanted to dance for Milli. Her eyes landed on a tall, thick chick with long hair that flowed down to her fat ass. She was wearing pasties with a pair of blue boy shorts trimmed in rhinestones. "Her."

Young Milli followed her finger and waved for Damu to come to him. "What's up?" Damu shouted over the music.

"Grab the chick in the blue, right there, and tell her I said come here."

"A'ight." Damu left the area and approached the chick. Milli could sense her excitement a mile away. Seconds later, she was standing in front of him. She leaned forward, so she could hear him and introduced herself as Sinnamon.

"I want you to give my lady a lap dance."

Milli watched as Sinnamon danced seductively on Aria's lap. From the looks of things, Aria seemed a bit apprehensive or perhaps nervous. He leaned over and whispered in her ear.

"Loosen up and have fun. It's just a dance. It don't mean you're gay."

"Okay, but I don't want you getting no ideas—or else." She made a gun with her fingers and pulled the trigger.

Milli understood exactly. But that was the furthest thing from his mind. He leaned back and watched Sinnamon bounce all of that ass on Aria's lap.

Slowly turning around to face Aria, Sinnamon stood between her legs and squatted with her hands on her knees and twerked, making her ass clap. Aria responded by throwing bills on her oily body.

Body-ody-ody-ody-ody-ody-ody-ody
Ody-ody-ody-ody-ody-ody-ody (mwah)
Body-ody-ody-ody-ody-ody-ody-ody (ah, ah, ah ah)
Ody-ody-ody-ody-ody-ody-ody

Megan Thee Stallion's song blared throughout the club. Sinnamon rapped along as she popped pussy and ass inches from Aria's face.

"Look at how I bodied that, ate it up and gave it back. Yeah, you look good, but they still wanna know where Megan at saucy like a barbecue but you won't get your baby back. See me in that dress and he feel like he almost tasted that."

On both sides of them, Young Milli's crew was turning up. Racks and racks of money was being thrown. To veteran eyes, those boys brought back memories of BMF, the Black Mafia Family led by the legendary Big Meech. The streets loved Young Milli because he was a true ATLien, straight from the Westside, and he hadn't forgotten where he came from. He repped the hood to the fullest.

The strippers loved him, too. Whenever he performed, the turnout was mad crazy and they were guaranteed to rake in a check. Add to that, Young Milli and his crew partied like rock stars and tipped the ladies generously. Tonight was no different. Other drug crews and rappers, along with their entourages tried to keep pace with Milli and his clique, which meant that the strippers were going to really cash in.

Money was all on the floor next to Sinnamon. It was much the same where Young Milli sat. He was being entertained by two strippers. A dozen or more were giving dances to his crew members.

Outside of the VIP section, Jaheim sipped on a glass of Henny as he eyed Young Milli and Aria. His mouth formed a straight line and his forehead was creased with wrinkles.

Beside him, Simona egged him on. "Go get your girl back from that nigga. Trust me, you're the one she really wants."

Jaheim's eyes told him a different story. But it didn't matter, because by now he was full of ego, jealousy, and the type of male pride that was as dangerous as a loaded gun in the hands of a spree killer.

He saw Aria dismiss the stripper that was dancing for her. Then, he saw the ladies that were dancing for Young Milli move on, too. Aria sat on Young Milli's lap, wrapped her arms around his neck and stuck her tongue in his mouth. Milli pulled out his phone and apparently started taking pictures of their shared kiss. From where he stood, Jaheim tried to study Aria's facial expression. She seemed unabashed.

Seeing that, Jaheim slung his drink against a wall. *We ain't been broken up a hot two weeks and this bitch all over this nigga! She probably been creeping with him all along.*

Now he was livid.

Ca$h & Destiny Skai

114

Chapter 17

Aria had no idea that she was being stalked. Every ounce of her attention was on Young Milli. She loved the way he showed her affection in public. She didn't know if what they had would last another week, month, or for a very long time. What she did know is that for the first time in her life she was totally happy. She wasn't looking too far down the road. *Just stay in the present*, she told herself.

She was in the middle of giving Milli a lap dance, when out of the blue, the vibe suddenly changed. The DJ went from spinning booty shaking club music to a slow jam at a wedding reception. The sweet voices of Jagged Edge filled the room, as Promise played softly through the speakers. Aria didn't know what to make of the drastic change, until Milli lifted her from his lap and stood. He motioned with two fingers in the air summoning someone over. Damu stepped close to them with a jewelry box in his hand.

As they stood facing one another, butterflies circulated throughout her belly and the rapid beat of her heart banged hard enough for her eardrums to rattle. *This can't be happening. This can't be happening.* All eyes were on them and it made her a nervous wreck. She could hardly breathe. Aria covered her mouth with both hands.

Nothing is promised to me and you. So why will we let this thing go? Baby, I promise that I'll stay true. Don't let nobody say it ain't so. And, baby, I promise. That I will never leave. And everything will be alright. I promise these things to you Girl, just believe. I promise.

Young Milli opened the box revealing a two carat diamond ring. "Aria, the past few days with you have been nothing short of amazing. Each day is always better than the last. This promise ring symbolizes what we're building together, one moment at a time. When you wear this ring, wear it with pride, and with the confidence that you are the *only* woman that's in my life. The *only* woman in this vast universe that's on a nigga's mind. With that being said, luv, please accept this ring with the promise that it's only you."

The scene was being shown on all the television screens throughout the club. Aria's heart was thumping like a drumbeat. The seconds that ticked by felt like minutes before she finally responded with her left hand out. She nodded her head with tears in her eyes and replied, "Yes."

The patrons clapped loudly. Some whistled with exuberance. Others seated nearby screamed out their congratulations. Phones were out as many people went live and snapped photos. "Congratulations, Young Milli and Aria," the DJ spoke on the mic. "May y'all commitment lead y'all back here soon for an engagement party hosted by me."

Milli graced her finger with the ring, followed with a passionate, yet erotic kiss. Just when she questioned the status of their relationship once she was back in Florida, he solidified her place in his life. Aria couldn't wait to thank Brandy for accepting the trip on her behalf.

"How did you pull this off?" she asked with knitted brows. Since their arrival he hadn't left the VIP section. Milli looked towards the DJ booth and nodded his head.

From outside the VIP room, Jaheim shot mean daggers in the their direction. What he'd just witnessed convinced him that the two had been creeping around for some time now. *Ain't no way this nigga serious after only spending a week with her. Fake ass Offset and Cardi B.* His thoughts were taken over by envy.

Simona placed her hand on his shoulder. "Damn, cousin, you alright?"

Jaheim freed himself from her touch. "What the fuck you think?"

He watched closely as Milli kissed her once more before heading on stage. The crowd was raucous, as they anticipated Young Milli performing his latest single *Turn Up In The Club.* The DJ hyped up the intro by screaming, "Ladies and gentlemen. Get out of your seats and welcome Atlanta's own Young Milli! Young Milli! Young muthafuckin' Milli! West Side in this muthafucka!"

The crowd erupted. Young Milli threw up his set and his homies went berserk. Aria watched him transform from the affectionate lover she knew into a boisterous, crotch grabbing, rap phenomenon that oozed magnetism. She loved this side of him, too. Because he loved it so much. And he was so fuckin' good at it. Almost as good at it as he was in bed.

"Whew!" Aria fanned herself. Just the thought of the things Young Milli did to her in the bedroom gave her a hot flash.

Before long, the liquor she had consumed filled her bladder. She hated to miss any part of Young Milli's performance, but she could not put off going to the restroom any longer. She had no idea who did he would encounter along the way.

Chapter 18

Aria slid out of the booth and went out into the main area of the club in search of the ladies room.

"Damn, shorty fine."

She could distinctively hear a group of men discussing how fine she was in her dress. One of them were bold enough to step to her, blocking her path. "Wassup, lil mama? Let a nigga get at you real quick."

"Excuse you." Throwing her hand up, she swatted him away like the annoying fly that he was, humming near her ear.

"Damn, I can't holla at you real quick?"

"I'm straight. Now, can you move?"

"I like 'em feisty," he grinned, exposing a mouth full of gold teeth. "Let a nigga take you to the Waffle House after the club."

Aria could smell a heavy combination of liquor and weed on his breath. He was drunk. She could tell by the way his words slurred. Finally, the crowd shifted, allowing her some space to walk away freely, leaving dude standing there with his mouth agape.

She wasn't interested in anything but the toilet, or any man that wasn't Milli, for that matter. Maneuvering through the crowd, a silver lining appeared when she saw the neon lights that read *ladies*. It felt like she had walked a green mile to get to where she was going.

Aria rushed through the door and into the stall with urgency, closing the door behind her. *Thank God it's clean in here*, she thought. As she relieved herself, she could hear two girls discussing how fine Milli was and their desire to have a one-night stand with him. Aria laughed on the inside and flushed the toilet.

There was a lady sitting at a table selling mints, perfume, and toiletries. You name it, she had it. The girls that were talking were now in the stall together. From the sound of the violent coughs, one of them had too much to drink. Aria washed her hands quickly. The sound of vomit made her stomach turn.

On her way down the dimly lit hall, someone snatched her by the arm. Aria spun on her heels with an attitude, ready to curse out the nigga that had violated her space.

"Let go of my fuckin'—" Aria froze when she saw that it was Jaheim, and Simona was behind him, smiling like a Cheshire cat.

"Hey, baby. I heard you've been missing me." Jaheim's mouth was dry.

"I most certainly have not. I don't know who told you that lie." Aria glared over his shoulder at Simona, correctly assuming that she was complicit in Jaheim being there.

"Aria, I just wanna talk to you," Jaheim pleaded.

"There is nothing for us to discuss. It's over, Jaheim. I've moved on. Goodbye and have a nice life." Aria tried to walk off but he grabbed a hold of her arm and yanked her back.

"Oh, you think you gon' dismiss me like I'm nobody?"

"You aren't anybody *to me*. Now, please let me go!" She swung with her free hand, slapping him upside the head.

Watching them go at it, Simona was almost giddy. "Kick that bitch's ass!" she instigated.

Aria tried to snatch away from Jaheim and attack Simona, but he had a vice grip on her arm, preventing her from moving. "Fuck that! You need to tell *me* something. Was you fuckin that nigga while we were together?"

"Who the hell are you to question me? Go question the bitch you got a baby with." Aria snapped. "Again, let go of me. I have to go chill with my man."

Jaheim gritted his teeth and breathed flames. "Bitch, how you curving me? I'm the same nigga whose dick you was sucking for two muthafuckin' years. Don't forget I used to nut in your mouth, ho'!"

Aria gasped. Her lips pursed, and before she knew it she had spat dead in Jaheim's face. "How dare you!" If her eyes were guns, she would've shot him dead.

Oh hell no! Beat her ass right now! Simona was rooting for more drama.

Jaheim wiped his face. As he did, flashbacks of their last conversation replayed in his mind, along with the videos and the public affection that played out in his face. The fire in Jaheim's eyes was strong enough to burn a hole through her soul. He pushed her against the wall and got right up in her face. They were close enough to kiss if he wanted to.

"Bitch, you got me fucked up. You been sucking and fucking on this nigga and bragging about it." He drew back to slap her, but a strong, powerful hand gripped his wrist.

"Aye, nigga, what the fuck you doing? Get yo' fuckin' hands off of her." Aria exhaled with a sigh of relief when she saw Damu come to her rescue with K-dog at his side.

Jaheim grilled Damu. He opened his mouth to say something but the words never came out. Damu knocked him out cold with one punch.

Twan saw Jaheim hit the floor, and he reacted immediately. Though he was seriously outsized against the two behemoths that had come to Aria's defense, that didn't stop him from swinging on Damu. He smashed him over the head with the champagne bottle he was holding. K-dog snatched Twan up and body slammed him to the floor. He and Damu started stomping mud holes in Jaheim and Twan.

Simona started backing up. This was not going as she had hoped.

A minute later, the club's security ran over and broke up the fracas. Knowing who Damu and K-dog rolled with, the bouncers didn't get aggressive with them. It was a different story in regards to Jaheim and Twan. Both of them were roughly escorted out of the club, bleeding and with knots on their heads. Simona had to run to keep up with them.

Inside the car, Twan retrieved his gun. He wanted to run up in the club and pop some lead in Damu, K-dog, and the bouncers that had put hands on them. The arrival of two marked police cruisers stopped him from going on a mission that would've resulted in many casualties.

"This shit ain't over!" he vowed.

"It's damn sho not!" Jaheim seconded as they left the scene. He, too, was as hot as a stolen pistol.

***

Young Milli didn't know anything about the altercation until he had finished performing and they were on their way home. His security was being super precautious and he wondered why. Damu, who was driving, recounted what had happened. Aria cut in to let it be known that the guy who was harassing her was her ex.

"Simona had to have something to do with him coming up here. Because she was with him," she explained.

"They better find somebody else to play with," Milli said.

That was all he said before he let it go. He didn't want anything to fuck up their mood. Aria didn't either. She had big plans for them for Christmas. It was finally here.

Chapter 19

Aria slipped from underneath a sleeping Milli, so she could start her day. It was Christmas morning and she had something particularly special planned for him. Milli had gone above and beyond for her and now it was time for him to receive the same treatment in return. Last night's event took the cake.

He was out of it right now, so the timing was perfect. Aria went into the bathroom to handle her hygiene. After a warm, refreshing shower, she dressed up in a short, sexy Santa baby doll dress. Then she went to the marble tub and ran a bubble bath, dropping rose petals on top of the bubbles, on the tile and to the door. There were a few things she needed from the kitchen, so she made a quick trip downstairs.

Milli was still asleep when she stepped back into the bedroom. Gently, she shook his shoulder, while admiring the rock on her finger once more.

"Wake up, sleepy head." He didn't move a muscle, so she tried again. "Bae, get up. I have something for you to see." Her voice elevated.

He stirred in his sleep and blinked several times to clear his vision. "What's up?"

"Merry Christmas, baby. Get up," she sang loudly while bouncing on the side of the bed.

"Merry Christmas," he stretched across the large bed and yawned at the same time. "What time is it?"

"Early, now get up. I have something special planned for you."

"Oh, yeah?" Milli rubbed his eyes and finally focused on the sexy outfit she was wearing. "Damn, bae," he groped her ass.

"You like my outfit?" Aria twirled in a circle. "I bought this just for you."

"Hell yeah! You lookin' like a sexy ass Mrs. Claus, or should I call you Ms. Milli Claus?" he laughed.

"I like Ms. Milli Claus better. Now, come on." Aria grabbed him by the hand and led him to the bathroom.

Milli smiled when he saw the rose petals and bottle of bubbly sitting on the side of the tub. "Okay, bae. I see you. I love it."

"You do, huh?"

"I love anything you do for me and to me." He winked, looking sexy as hell. It was easy to be distracted, so she tried her best to stay on task.

"Get naked."

"You getting in with me?"

"Nope. I just want you to relax and sip on the champagne," she nodded towards the tub. "Then I'm going to come back and bathe you."

"G-shit?" he grinned.

"G-shit, baby," she mocked him playfully.

"Oh, okay. I see you, bae." He rubbed his hands together. "We on that Prince Akeem, Coming to America shit, huh? He's the king of Zamunda, but I'm the king of Atlanta."

"You can say that," she giggled. "Get comfortable and I'll be right back."

While Milli relaxed, Aria used that time to set up the massage table, light some candles from Bath and Body Works, and drop another trail of rose petals from the bedroom to the bathroom. Once that was complete, she went back to the kitchen to start on their breakfast. Milli's personal chef prepped their food the day before making it easier for Aria.

For thirty minutes, she sipped on some champagne while getting the food together. On the menu was shrimp, grits, eggs, and biscuits. According to the chef, it was one of his favorite morning dishes. The aroma of the food made her stomach growl in pain. Alcohol without food equaled a stomachache. *Chill out girl, we gone eat.* She rubbed her flat belly.

Aria returned to the bathroom and washed Milli thoroughly. He enjoyed every second of it. She did her best to ignore the tip of his head peeking through the bubbles. "The royal penis is clean, Your Highness."

They both laughed at the line she quoted from *Coming to America.*

Milli stepped out of the tub and dried himself off. "I ain't have a penis since elementary school." He gripped his meat through the towel he was wearing. "This all dick right here. Grade A beef."

"Hmm, you right about that." Aria turned on her heels and left the bathroom with Milli trailing behind her.

"Bae, what is all of this?"

"I'm about to give you a massage, so climb up on the table."

As soon as he was comfortable, Aria put the flat screen television on YouTube and selected some meditation music. The sounds of waves crashing on the beach filled the room. She began the massage by sprinkling warm drops of oil on his back, arms, and legs and worked her magic on his sexy body for one hour. She spent thirty minutes on his back and the equal amount on his chest. His perfectly drawn tattoos were truly amazing as they glistened. The one she admired the most was the drawing of his mother. She was absolutely beautiful.

Aria worked her way down to his stomach and did her best to stay focused, but she couldn't resist. The dip underneath his belly button drove her crazy. It was like his body was calling her name. Milli had become her drug and she was addicted.

So, addicted that she couldn't wait to taste him again. She took his semi-stiff rod into her mouth and sucked it slowly until it stretched to its full potential, hitting the back of her throat. Passionately, she bobbed up and down at a slow pace, savoring his pre-cum.

"Ohh, shit, bae," he grunted in a weak tone and grabbed a handful of her hair. "Suck that dick just like that."

Aria spit on the tip and slurped on it aggressively. Milli damn near snatched a plait out of her scalp, but that didn't stop her from putting in that work.

Minutes later, she could feel his warm cum ooze to the back of her throat. That was the appetizer, now it was time for the main course.

Aria removed the food from the warmer and fixed their plates. "Breakfast for my king." She sat down a dish for Milli and one for herself.

Milli grabbed her effortlessly by the wrist, pulling her towards him. "Thanks, luv. I appreciate everything you doing to make a nigga feel special. It's been eleven years since a woman catered to me."

"You're welcome, baby. I just want to see you happy."

"Well, you're doing a good job of it."

Aria rocked side to side. "Would you be upset if I didn't get you anything for Christmas? I mean you have everything, so I didn't know what to get you."

Milli watched her eyes for a moment before he responded. He wasn't pressed about a gift. Having Aria with him was a gift within itself. "It's cool, luv. Don't sweat that. I have everything I need right here. You cooking and catering to me is more than enough and I've enjoyed every minute of it."

Breakfast was slamming. Milli ate everything on his plate and Aria was happy about that. All she could hear was her mother's voice. *Baby, the way into a man's heart is through his stomach.* She collected Milli's plate, sat it in the sink, and sashayed back to where he was sitting. "Are you ready for your special dessert?" she asked with heavy seduction in her words.

"Hell yeah!" Milli knew exactly what she was referring to.

Aria removed the place mat from in front of him and sat on the table with her knees up to her breast. Milli leaned forward and put his face in the place. Slowly, he flickered his tongue up and down her creases before nibbling on her pearl.

Aria grabbed the back of his head, while thrusting her hips upward. She yearned to feel the stroke of his tongue. "Ahhh. Yeah, baby. Just like that."

Milli used his right hand to free his dick from the restraints of his boxer briefs and stroke it while sending Aria to ecstasy. Once she was nice and wet and he was standing at attention, he rose to his feet and pulled her back to the edge of the table. Teasing her, he smacked his meat against her middle and rubbed the head between her petals. He had her anxious. "Daddy, put it in please," she begged.

Succumbing to her pleas, he pushed his way deep inside the warmth of her walls. "Hold your legs open for daddy." Aria rotated her hips and grabbed her ankles.

Milli placed both hands on her waistline and thrust his hips at a steady, slow pace. He wanted to make love to her body and capture her soul. "Arghh," he growled. "You got me ready to bust already." Her pussy gripped his steel tightly. He was on the verge of busting prematurely, but he wasn't ready yet. Milli stopped mid-stroke and held his head back for a seconds, until he felt that urge fade away.

"Not yet," she whispered.

Milli shook the feeling and watched his rod disappear and reappear with every stroke. Aria wrapped her legs around his waist and met him halfway with each thrust. She could feel her second orgasm building up. "Unt un! Pick 'em back up," he said in between grunts, switching up the pace.

"I want you to make me cum," she confessed.

"I got you, baby," he promised and tapped her G-spot.

"Oooh. Keep it right there. Fuck me, daddy. Just like that," she squealed feeling him deep in her guts. "Make me cum. Make me cum," she begged.

Milli planted his thumb on top of her clit and stroked her into a heavy orgasm. "Cum for me, baby. Cream all over this dick." His rod was coated in her juices. Her body trembled like a fiend. Aria's legs felt numb and collapsed at his waist, but he pushed them apart. "Keep 'em open." Her body was in relax mode.

Milli drew back just a little and rammed his inches from side to side. His balls smacked against her booty. That snapped her out of her laziness when he hit those corners. Aria used her arms to keep her knees planted against her chest. She kept that position until he reached his climax with one final, powerful thrust.

"Damn," Aria exhaled and rocked her legs from side to side. "Look at how you do me."

"Look at how you wet up my table," Milli joked.

"Consider that as me marking my territory." Aria sat up and damn near slid off of the table.

"Well, you have about eleven more rooms to mark. So, you better get your energy up fuckin' with me."

"Whatever. Let's go upstairs," she insisted. There were a few more things that she had up her sleeve.

Back in the bedroom, Milli stretched across the bed and waited for Aria to return with another surprise. To him, she had done enough and he was satisfied.

Aria got his attention when she crossed the threshold bearing presents. "Bae, you didn't have to buy me any gifts."

"I know that, but I wanted to do this for you. You've done so much for me and I just felt like I should do the same." Aria sat the bags next to him.

"Everything I did was from the heart. I did it to make you happy. Not for me to receive something in return."

"That's no different from what I did for you," she said sweetly and handed him the first gift of many. "Start with this one first." She pointed.

Milli tore off the wrapping paper and opened the box. Staring back at him was a black Versace Palazzo watch. He nodded his head. "Oh, yeah, this is tight. I love it. Thanks, baby."

"Don't thank me yet. There's more where that came from."

Aria watched as Milli opened up all of his gifts. The huge smile on his face made her happy that she chose to spend her six-thousand dollar Christmas bonus on him.

"There's one more gift that I have for you to open, but I have to record your reaction. This gift was made with pure, authentic love."

"Okay." For a second, Milli thought he was about to open up a pregnancy test. But he quickly dismissed that idea since she'd only been there a week and there was no way she could know that already.

Aria grabbed her cellphone from the dresser and handed him his last gift. Once again, he tore off the paper and prepared himself for the ultimate surprise. Milli saw that it was another jewelry box and opened it. It was a gold Cuban link necklace with a circle medallion trimmed in diamonds. The piece was nice, but the photo on it was what truly stole his heart. It was a picture of him and his First Lady. His mother, the late Deidre Harris.

Milli stared at the chain for a few seconds. His thumb outlined the photo several times. Bringing his hand up to his nose, he closed his eyes.

Yeah Mama, she's definitely the one.

Chapter 20

Aria was just as sure that Young Milli was the one for her. This past week had her floating on a cloud. Nothing would ever be able to top the pampering she'd received from Milli on a daily basis ever since she agreed to visit him. It was so true that being with a worthless dog of a man, like Jaheim, had been blocking her blessings, she realized.

Thank God I had the sense and the conviction to delete him from my life.

She felt truly blessed to have a real man in her cipher now. She didn't question if she deserved him. Aria knew that she was a prize, too. She was attractive, intelligent, independent and, most of all, faithful and loyal. So, she wasn't coming to the table with nothing but a fork in her hand. She was bringing the main course, which was a woman that a man could build an empire with. She knew how to wear her crown, adjust it if need be, or take it off and whoop a bitch ass if that's what the situation called for. Whatever it took to protect her man, Aria was game for it. As long as that man was worth the mighty, mighty love she had to give. Young Milli was damn sure worth it in Aria's eyes.

"Baby, you ready?" he asked, ending a phone call that had momentarily interrupted their evening.

"Yes, my king." She stood up and took his arm.

Dressed in matching ugly sweaters, they were headed to a Christmas dinner, sponsored by Young Milli, for his entire crew and their ladies. Aria was still a bit tired from their long lovemaking session earlier in the day, but she was a soldier. She would've gotten out of bed and hopped on a space shuttle to the moon, as long as she was with Milli.

At the spacious ballroom where the dinner was being held, Aria saw that everyone was wearing ugly sweaters. All of the men had a lady on their arm, even Milli's three main goons. Seeing Damu and them in this atmosphere humanized them to her. They were much more relaxed and personable than when they were fulfilling their roles as bodyguards and henchmen. They introduced her to their lady friends as *Milli's woman* and none of the women gave her the side-eye. When she was left alone with the ladies, she was pleased that they weren't the gossiping-type. Judging from their conversation, they all seemed to have their own businesses or careers. That told her a lot about the type of men Young Milli affiliated himself with.

True to Young Milli's style, he went overboard with the food. Dinner was an eleven course meal beginning with an appetizer of light finger foods. Then, a light soup followed by fish, turkey and dressing, vegetables, punch, a delicious roast, chowder, salad, an assortment of cold dishes, a second entree, dessert, cheese and fruit, and finally liquor and Cuban cigars for the men in the banquet's den, and wine and finger snacks for the women in a beautifully decorated drawing room.

The evening ended with a performance by the Braxtons. Toni brought the house down.

Aria was living a whole dream. But a nightmare was right around the corner.

Chapter 21

Christmas was a blast. Aria did her thing with the massage and gifts, and the dinner turned out just as Milli had hoped it would. But for some reason that he couldn't explain, Milli hadn't slept well that night. He tossed and turned until the sun came up. When he opened his eyes, Milli saw Aria laying on her side with her head propped up on her hand.

"Bae, you slept rough last night," she said, concerned.

"I know, but I'm good." He rolled over, gave her a quick kiss, and headed to the bathroom. "When is your flight?" he called back to her.

"Tomorrow, the twenty-seventh."

"Can you change it to the second of January? I wanna fly you to New York to bring New Year's in with me."

"Okay, babe. I can do that. I'm not due back to work until the fifth."

"Change your return flight to the fourth, then. Unless that won't give you enough time to get ready to go back to work." Milli was shouting to her from the bathroom, while he took a leak.

When he came back into the bedroom after washing his hands, Aria told him that the fourth would be just fine. She wasn't ready to leave him, either. In fact, she had been dreading her vacation coming to the end. Now that they knew they had another week together before Aria had to return home, they both could relax.

"After I do this show tonight, I'ma take a break from performing for a while. After a trip to New York, we're going to Colorado. We're gonna get a cabin and chill in front of a big ass fireplace, maybe play in the snow or have a snowball fight. Just you and me," said Young Milli.

"Colorado? Yes!" Aria got excited. "Can we go skiing while we're there?"

"Now, you know a nigga from the hood don't know how to ski," he laughed.

"I've never been skiing, either, but we can learn together. Please, bae." she hugged his arm and looked up at him.

"I'll give it a try. Just for you."

"You're everything," she beamed.

"So are you, luv." Milli kissed her and rubbed her booty.

Aria took that as a sign that she was about to get some of that good morning wood, but Milli told her he had to hit the streets and handle some business. He suggested that she go shopping to buy an outfit to wear to Diamond's, the club where he was performing tonight.

"No, bae. I have plenty of outfits I can choose from right here." She refused to let him buy her anything else.

"It's nothing, though. I love doing things for you. A man spoils whoever is special to him. For me, that's you. So, let me do what I do." He looked at her and licked his lips. That shit was so sexy, Aria wanted to jump his bones even though he had things to do.

Normally, she would give in to whatever he wanted, but this time she stood her ground. She didn't need a new dress or anything that money could buy. Milli asking her to stay another week was everything in and of itself. "Not." She wagged her finger in finality.

"A'ight, you got that, luv," Milli relented.

Once Milli left the house, Aria called Brandi and they caught up on the last couple of days. Brandi was so happy for her girl. She told her that she deserved every drop of happiness that she was experiencing.

"I think you're in love," Brandi teased.

134

"I am," Aria shamelessly admitted. "I know it sounds silly, being that we haven't known each other long, but there's no set length of time to fall in love."

"Right. My mother said she fell in love with my dad the first time she ever saw him. And they've been together almost forty years."

Aria prayed that she and Milli's story would play out similarly, but she had no plans of crowding him. She would visit him when it was convenient for both of them, and she wouldn't nag, complain, or question him about how he moved. As long as he continued to show her that she was the woman he wanted, she would let that man handle his business. If the day came where he showed her otherwise, she promised herself she would be strong enough to walk away gracefully. When she expressed those sentiments to Brandi, her bestie said, "Girl, ain't no nigga doing all of what Young Milli has done for you if he didn't see you as the one to hold on to."

"More than the things he's given me, I can see the sincerity in his eyes. I can feel it in his touch. If I'm wrong, he's a better actor than Will Smith, Denzel, Jamie Foxx and all the others," Aria surmised.

Unconsciously, she looked down at the promise ring on her finger. *When you wear this ring, wear it with pride, and with the confidence that you are the only woman that's in my life. The only woman in this vast universe that's on a nigga's mind.* Young Milli's heartfelt promise played in Aria's mind, assuring her that her love for him would not end in heartbreak.

Hours later, they were still on the phone. Aria told Brandi about Jaheim showing up at the club on Christmas Eve and confronting her. "And that trick cousin of mine, Simona, was with him."

"*Whaattt?*" Brandi sang, correctly interpreting Simona's part in Jaheim being there.

"Yup. I should've knocked that bitch the fuck out like Damu did Jaheim."

They both burst out in laughter.

***

One person who wasn't laughing was Twan.

Being a young hitta, who refused to wear a beat down and chalk it up as a bad night, was out for revenge. That's all he had been talking about since the night it happened. He had even managed to pump Jaheim up to get on some gangsta shit.

At first, Jaheim was just going to take the L and keep it moving, but Twan challenged his manhood. "Unc, if you let another nigga beat you down and I don't get back at him, I'ma lose all respect for you. Nigga, you from the bricks, the projects, just like me. A nigga touch us, we touch them back! And like I said before we left Florida, the broad can get it, too. She started all of this."

By the time Twan finished talking, Jaheim was gassed up. He was almost to the point of hating Aria. She had made him look like a duck. And he couldn't just take an ass kicking and not do shit about it, or he wouldn't be able to show his face in the hood again. Twan would tell all of the homeboys what went down.

"How you plan on getting to them?" asked Jaheim. "You see how deep they roll."

"We can catch 'em at that club where Young Milli is performing tonight. It's been all over his IG page. I'ma wait on them to come out the club when it's over. That's when I'ma strike. All you gotta do is drive. I'ma dump on all of those niggas." Twan had it all planned out. Though Jaheim was much older than him, he took a backseat to Twan when it came to that rah rah shit.

***

The day passed by quickly. Before Young Milli knew it, it was time to head to Diamond's. The establishment wasn't upscale. Rather, it was hood, and the doorman was notoriously for having a relaxed attitude about allowing people to enter without searching them for weapons. All a nigga had to do was slide them a few bills and the doormen would wave them right on in. That was a major concern. The streets were saying that BNK and his crew were planning to come to the club and set it off. Young Milli didn't believe BNK was built like that, but he knew not to ever underestimate anybody.

Milli had discussed what the streets were saying with his security team and the rest of his squad who were rolling with him tonight. Everybody would be strapped up. They were riding in a twenty car convoy of different foreign whips tonight. Showing up and showing out. Milli didn't want to be chauffeured on this occasion. It was time for him to break in the red 2022 Porsche 911 Carrera Cabriolet that he had parked in the garage. Tonight would be the first time he whipped it out. Having Aria in the passenger seat would enhance the luxury of the high-end sports car. Although he was driving himself to the club, Milli felt safe behind the bulletproof windows he had gotten installed in the vehicle.

***

It was the average night at a club where Young Milli was performing. The crowd was thick, the women were out in abundance, and the ballers were doing what they do—partying like the hood stars they were. Aria was in VIP, sipping a daiquiri and watching her man rip the mic.

On this night, Young Milli was at his absolute mesmerizing best.

He had been on stage for twenty minutes longer than planned, but the crowd kept screaming for more. Sweat dripped from his body, as he put one hundred percent passion into his performance.

Out the corner of his eye, he saw a rustle in the crowd, then all of a sudden BNK and more than a dozen of his soldiers rushed the stage.

Young Milli reached for his waist, but he had given his pipe to one of his mans to hold before going on stage. One of BNK's homies snatched the mic from Young Milli and gave it to BNK, who immediately announced, "I'm the king of ATL! Fuck Young Milli and his whole crew! I'm the Bitch Nigga Killa. I'm about to murder this bitch nigga on the mic!"

Before BNK could spit one line, Young Milli had coldcocked the nigga that snatched the mic, and he was headed at BNK. Another dude with BNK flashed his steel. "Nigga, you must wanna die!" he snarled.

Young Milli didn't give a fuck about that nigga's gun, he was about to test his gangsta. He shoved the dude in the chest with two hands and then he felt two thuds in his own chest.

Pwwwt! Pwwwt!

The silencer on the gun muffled the sound, but the impact of the bullets caused Young Milli to stumble back and fall. The guy hid his gun down by his side, jumped off of the stage and disappeared into the crowd. Young Milli lay on his back, struggling to get back to his feet.

He looked up and saw that the calvary was on the way.

Xmas in the Arms of an ATL Shooter

***

Damu and the crew was on the move. They reached the stage in packs. Fights broke out on stage and then throughout the club. In the blink of an eye, it was bedlam. Niggas *and* bitches were getting laid out, some for no reason at all. K-dog was beating one of those BNK clowns half to death. Damu tossed one nigga after the other off stage as he made his way to Young Milli, who was fighting two fools.

In the middle of the melee, BNK was still rapping. Another one of his people was on IG live, showing the ongoing fight, clout chasing until Mob Slim broke his jaw.

Although, the IG live ended, the brawl was just getting cracking. Not everyone with BNK was soft. Particularly, a guy named Scrap. As Damu ran past him on stage, he shoved a knife in Damu's chest. "Bitch nigga!" Scrap snarled.

A stream of blood squirted from Damu's chest and he fell to his knees reaching for his banger. Scrap stood over him and plunged the knife in his chest again. Reflexively, Damu squeezed the trigger of the gun that was halfway out of his waist, before he fell forward on his face and bled out.

The distinctive sound of a gunshot caused pandemonium. There was a mad rush for the door. Then a bevy of gunshots. *Boc! Boc! Boc! Boom! Boom! Boom! Boom! Blocka! Blocka! Blocka! Blocka!*

Patrons were trampled as they tried to flee outside. Having been saved by his bpv, Young Milli made it to his feet. He dropped an opp with a punch to the chin, hopped off stage and fought through the madness, in search of Aria.

"Aria! Aria!" he shouted.

Even over the screams, gunfire and her own cries, Aria heard Young Milli shouting her name. "Milli! Over here! I'm over here, bae!" She called back, as tears poured down her face. She held up her arms, hoping against all hope that he would see her, and find his way to her, but she was being swept toward the exit by the tidal wave of bodies surrounding her. Everyone was in a panic except the two warring sides.

Scrap kicked Damu in the head but he didn't feel it, he had already crossed over to the other side. K-dog saw it, though. He ran up to Scrap and shot him dead between the eyes. Scrap was deceased before his body hit the stage floor. Still, K-dog put five bullets in his chest.

By now, the stage was cleared out. BNK blended his fat ass in with the crowd, surrounded by several of his homies. It was a good thing that he was close to the door, because Young Milli had gotten a hold of a gun and he was pushing through the frantic crowd, looking for his main adversary.

Chapter 22

Jaheim and Twan were parked in the club's parking lot when they saw everyone running outside. "What the fuck?" said Twan.

Sitting behind the wheel of the car, Jaheim rolled down the windows to hear what was going on.

"They're shooting in there!" He heard several people say as they ran by his car. He started the engine and reached for the gear shift, thinking that with all the commotion going on there was no way they would locate their targets.

"No!" said Twan, gripping Jaheim's wrist. "This shit is perfect. They gotta come out now."

Twan got out of the car and leaned against the front side panel. His gat was in his hand, hidden inside his jacket. As soon as he spotted Young Milli or either of the dudes that had stomped him out, he was busting off.

People were everywhere, shouting, crying, running. A couple of people were laying on the ground bleeding. Twan eyes got big when he spotted Aria. He didn't see Young Milli or either of those big ass niggas with her.

He waited a few seconds, gun ready, and then an idea quickly formed in his mind. In a flash, he moved towards her.

***

Aria was standing there, worrying about her man. Her arms were wrapped around her shoulders and she was shivering from the cold. Suddenly, she felt someone shove a hard object in her side. She looked down and saw that it was a gun.

"Walk with me to the car, bitch, and you better not scream! If you make a sound I'ma kill yo' ass right here!" threatened Twan.

Aria thought about running but he had her by the arm, pulling her along with him. "Who are you?" she cried. She didn't recognize Twan from the other night.

"You'll find out soon enough."

When they got to the car, Aria screamed, "Help! Help! Somebody help!" But with all that was going on outside the club, no one heard her cries.

Twan slapped her with the gun, knocking her unconscious. Then, he slung her limp body in the backseat and hopped in beside Aria. "Mash out!" he barked.

Jaheim hesitated, but only for a second. Snatching Aria hadn't been part of the plan. But it was too late to back out now, he told himself. *In for a dime in for a dollar.* He put the car in gear and floored it.

***

Young Milli searched for Aria frantically, but she was nowhere to be found. He called her phone but there was no answer. He left a voicemail. "Baby, where are you? Answer your phone! I need to know you're okay. Call me back asap!" He hung up and tried to gather up his team, but most of them had fled the scene. Police were all over the place now.

Mob Slim found Milli posted up in the parking lot across from Diamond's. He pulled up to him and rolled down the window. "Milli, we gotta get out of here!"

"Where's everyone at?"

"They all went to the spot," he said, referring to the place they'd usually meet up when there was trouble. "Damu didn't make it though. Homie is dead."

"What you mean?" Milli hadn't seen Damu get stabbed. Mob Slim quickly told him what happened. "He's gone, fam. I rolled him over. And I heard him take his last breath." A tear for his fallen comrade fell from his eye. "K-dog smashed the nigga that did it. And I slumped two of those niggas," he reported.

Young Milli closed his eyes briefly and dropped his head. *Damn, bro, I'm sorry.* Although he knew how the game went, and so did Damu, that shit hit differently when it actually happened; when you lose one of your people. Milli felt the loss in his heart.

"Did we lose anybody else?" he asked.

"I don't know yet. Boss man, we gotta go. They're gonna start setting up roadblocks and we not tryna get caught in that shit. I'm dirty."

"Go on to the spot. I'll be there." Milli tossed his iron in Mob Slim's lap, and walked across the street to where several ambulances were. He wanted to be there when they brought Damu out. He didn't want his mans to be alone, especially in death. Also, he couldn't leave until he found Aria.

The police ordered the crowd in the parking lot to move back as they marked off a large area at the front of the club with yellow and black crime scene tape. They began loading the wounded into ambulances. The bodies of five people who were deceased weren't brought out until hours later. From the size of the body they brought out last, Young Milli knew it was Damu even though he was covered with a white sheet.

Blood, I'ma ride for you. Nothing but death can stop me.

As Damu's body was being driven away. Young Milli continued to search the lot for Aria and call her phone. Finally, someone answered but it wasn't Aria.

"I got your bitch. If you wanna get her back alive it's gonna cost you a hundred bands. Get the bread together. I'll be in touch. And if you call the po's she's dead." The unfamiliar male on the other end of the phone disconnected the call.

Young Milli found his car, hopped inside and started for home to get the money together. Before he could get a half mile from the club he was caught in a roadblock. Once his identity became known, he was detained and taken to the police station to be questioned.

With every moment that ticked by, he worried that Aria was going to be killed.

***

Young Milli invoked his right to remain silent. He didn't answer a single question the police asked. He wasn't belligerent towards them, knowing that would only give them reason to *find* something to charge him with, but he had no rap for them. They tested his hands for traces of gun powder, but found none. When they asked how his bulletproof vest came to be damage, he replied, "Again, I invoke my right to an attorney."

The investigator was already pushing his luck. By the letter of the law, he was supposed to have ended the interrogation the first time Young Milli requested an attorney. This time, the investigator adhered to the law. "Okay, you can go. But you'll be seeing me again, soon enough. And if there's any retaliation in the streets, I'll personally come to arrest you," he threatened.

"Am I free to go?" Young Milli calmly asked.

"Get the fuck out of my station!"

Young Milli stood up and walked out without uttering a response. He had more important things to deal with. Things that wore heavily on his heart.

Chapter 23

Two days passed without Young Milli hearing from the kidnappers. He couldn't eat or sleep, and he looked ragged.

"I gotta find my girl," he kept saying. "And we gotta ride for Damu. Them niggas gotta pay for that. Their mommas gon' cry, too."

He let out a long sigh. The recent events were really testing his composure. Especially after he had seen Damu's body in the morgue earlier today. Young Milli had almost broken down.

Damu had been much more than his top shooter and goon. He had been a loyal friend and a trusted confidante. Milli couldn't recall a single time where Damu questioned any of his decisions. He demonstrated no sign of jealousy or envy towards Young Milli.

As Milli and the crew smoked and reminisced about their fallen brother, Milli particularly recalled something Damu had told him after one of their close associates and his entire family had gotten murdered.

Milli had asked, *"Is this what it's all about, blood? Burying homies at a young age? Innocent people getting killed just because they fuck with niggas like us? We kill some opps, they kill some of us, then we strike back. It's like it's a big circle."*

"That's what we signed up for. And you being the shot caller, it's harder on you, because you blame yourself when one of us bites the dust. Heavy is the head that wears the crown."

"You said that shit right," Young Milli uttered now. Because this was a heavy ass load to carry. He blew a cloud of smoke up in the air. "You was a real one, blood. A true friend. Death to all those niggaz. I promise you that."

No sooner than those words came out of Young Milli's mouth did his phone ring. He didn't recognize the number, but he was answering every call just in case it was Aria's abductors calling.

"Hello?"

"You got that bread ready?"

***

As soon as Twan got the answer he was hoping to hear, he gave Young Milli detailed instructions on where to leave the $100,000. When he hung up the phone, he turned to Jaheim, who was sitting on the bed. "If you haven't heard from me in an hour and a half, you know what to do."

"I hear you," replied Jaheim. To Twan's ears it sounded like he was wavering.

Twan looked him sternly in the eyes. "I don't care what you feel about her, do what you gotta do. Ya feel me? If I come back with the money, you won't have to get blood on your hands."

"Cool." Jaheim hoped things went off without a hitch because he didn't think he could take Aria's life. He was mad as fuck at her, but not mad enough to kill her.

"A'ight. I'm out. And leave that bitch tied up. Don't take no chances," Twan reiterated.

"I'm not. Be careful, lil bruh," said Jaheim.

"Fa sho." Twan went off to get that bag.

Aria was tied to a chair, blindfolded, and a strip of duct tape covered her mouth. She had been in this same position for more than forty-eight hours. Periodically, the tape had been removed from over her mouth for them to give her water, and she'd been taken to the bathroom twice. Otherwise, she had been held hostage in the chair. Every muscle and bone in her body ached. She kept asking herself how did she end up in this position. Was she to blame? Or Young Milli? Would this be happening to her had she never decided to visit him?

Constant thoughts of the pandemonium that broke out in the club played out in her mind. It was the scariest moment in Aria's life. From ducking bullets to having a gun shoved in her ribcage was traumatizing. Being hit with the gun was painful, but she was grateful to be alive. But for how long?

Aria was certain that they were going to kill her after Young Milli paid the ransom. That's what happened in the movies. Aria had nothing else to reference. Tears began to soak the cloth blindfold that covered her eyes. *How could this really be happening?* she asked herself. No, she couldn't blame Young Milli, he had done everything in his power to love on her and protect her. The only persons to blame were her kidnappers, one of whom she would've never thought could do this to her. No matter how acrimonious things had become between them.

Aria hadn't been able to place the voice of the other guy, but she was certain Jaheim was one of them. Not only had she recognized his car when she was being dragged toward it, she had heard him talking, and his voice was as familiar to her as the back of her own hand.

Aria recalled a time when he was her first thought in the morning and her last thought before she closed her eyes at night. She remembered a time when she gave him reason to believe in himself. There had been a time when he loved her the best he knew how.

Could he really take my life? Has things become that bad?

Aria rocked back and forth in the chair until she got Jaheim's attention.

"Bathroom?" he asked. trying to disguise his voice. Aria shook her head *no*. "Water?"

She nodded *yes*.

Jaheim grabbed a bottle of water out of the small fridge, walked over to her and gently removed the tape from over her mouth. The other guy would've just ripped it off. She was thankful he wasn't there.

"Jaheim, why are you doing this?" She spoke on weak breath.

"That ain't my fuckin' name!"

"Jah, I know it's you." She hoped that her calling him by the pet name would stir fond memories in his mind.

"Oh, it's Jah now?" he bristled. "It wasn't *Jah* when you was curving me for a brand new nigga you haven't known but a hot fuckin' minute!"

"I wasn't curving you." Aria cried harder. "Don't you think I have the right to be happy?" she sobbed.

"Don't cry tears, they don't fly here!" He sounded heartless, but Aria didn't know him to be that way. Yeah, he was unfaithful and a habitual liar, but she had never known him to be flat out cold-hearted.

"Please uncover my eyes," she pleaded.

"For what?"

"So, I can look in your eyes."

"Hell no!"

"Please, Jah. I'm not no bitch in the streets. This is Aria you're doing this to. The same woman who gave you a chance when you were down and out." She sniffled, and tears ran down into her mouth as she tried to reason with him.

"And the same woman who gave up on me and replaced me a day or two later. Then, you all over social media with that nigga, like he's better than me. Fuck you, Aria. Whatever has happened to you, you deserved that shit. Facts!"

"Okay. If that's how you really feel take this blindfold off of me and look me in the eyes and tell me I deserve it. Can you do that? That's my one request. Please do that for me."

It was quiet for a moment before he responded. "I'll do you that one good, but it ain't gonna change nothing." He figured his half of the $100,000 was compensation for Young Milli taking Aria from him.

Jaheim removed the blindfold from over Aria's eyes.

"Thank you," she said.

Jaheim nodded his head and looked into her eyes. The disappointment he saw in her face disarmed him a bit, but the anger in him fueled him. "I'm looking in your eyes and ain't nothing changed. You still gonna be here until lil homie gets back with that dough. You just better hope your boyfriend don't renege." If that happened, he wasn't sure if he would be able to stop Twan from hurting her.

Aria feared that Jaheim's partner might kill her even after Young Milli paid the ransom. She knew she had to talk some sense in Jaheim, appeal to his heart, because he had obviously lost his mind. She blinked her eyes, adjusting to the light. Then, she spoke from the heart. "Jah, how could you claim to love me, but allow someone else to hurt me?"

"*Loved*. Not love," he corrected her.

"Real love is forever," she said.

"Fuck outta here! You didn't love me forever."

Aria explained that she did indeed still love him although she was no longer in love with him. "I dedicated two years to you. I was there when everyone else flaked on you. I held you down when you had nothing." Tears filled her eyes and made a slow trail down her cheeks. "I loved you with every fiber in my body and you cheated, over and over again. You had me questioning my own attractiveness and self-worth. Then, you got with Mya and had an outside baby. And you knew that becoming a mother is something I really wanted, but God hasn't gave me that blessing yet and maybe He never will. But, when you had a baby with another woman, that crushed me, Jah. I had to walk away. So, you can't blame me for choosing my happiness first. You broke me and now you're doing it again." Aria was bawling loudly and time was ticking.

Chapter 24

Twan couldn't believe how easily that had gone. After getting the bag out of the dumpster, he'd walked briskly back to the car and looked inside the small backpack. It was full of neatly stacked 20's, 50's and 100's. He let out a long, excited yell and thought of what he would do with the money. He wanted to buy so many things. *I should've demanded a quarter mil'. They don't call that nigga Young Milli for nothing.*

Twan realized that he wouldn't have but $50,000 after he split the money with Jaheim. *Fifty bands won't last no time. Plus, I'ma be ducking Young Milli. It takes more than fiddy thou' to go somewhere and get established like I want to.*

He also knew that he might have to run from the police. Because he was about to catch a body. There was no way he was going to allow Aria to live. He just didn't trust her not to go to the police if they let her go. He didn't think he would have to worry about that with Young Milli. *He's a street nigga, he'll try to handle this shit with street justice,* Twan thought.

As he headed back to the hotel, he kept a steady eye on his rearview mirror, making sure he wasn't being followed. The duffle bag was on his lap, he had one hand on the steering wheel and the other hand gripped his banger. Nothing and no one was going to separate him from this bag. To Twan, it was the come-up of a lifetime.

***

"I would've gave you a lifetime had you treated me right and been faithful. You destroyed what we had, Jah, not me," Aria managed to say through her balling.

"I don't believe that shit. You didn't love me," he replied.

"Jah, do you hear yourself?" Aria said. "Come here. Hold my hands." Her arms were bound together at the wrist, but she opened her hands.

"We ain't gotta do all that," he said weakly.

"Please. Do it for me."

He sat the bottle of water down and took her hands in his. "This wasn't apart of the plan, Aria." Jaheim sighed. His eyes weren't on Aria, they were on the floor. "I'm sorry. This wasn't supposed to go down like this. I came here to try and get you back, but everything went left after the fight. This nigga wanted revenge against your new boyfriend and you were just a casualty. It's all about the money with him. Nothing more, nothing less."

"Jah, just let me go, please. I promise that I won't call the police on you. I swear. And I won't let Milli come after you. You have my word on that. I just want this craziness to end."

"I can't do that. I'm no longer running the show. The dynamics changed once that nigga's hittas jumped us in the club. That young boy ain't hearing nothing else."

Aria squeezed his hands, pleading. "How could you let this go down like this? That's not the man I know. That's not the man your mother raised. You going to let another man make decisions for you? I was there for your mother when you thought you were going to lose her due to COVID. I made sure she ate and had everything that she needed. How do you think she would feel knowing that you didn't protect me? If you don't love me, she does. Are you going to let him kill a part of her?"

For the first time in minutes, he looked at her. Aria could see the sadness in his eyes.

"Aria, I do love you. I've always loved you. I just didn't know how to love you properly. Mya was just a chick I was smashing on the side and she ended up pregnant. I don't love

154

her and I have no desire to be with her, but you put me out. I didn't have anywhere else to go, so I went to her place."

"If you love me you would let me go. This isn't you and I know that."

"You know I would never hurt you."

"I know that, but would you let him hurt me?"

He sat in silence, staring into her eyes. Remembering that Aria was the one who gave him the down payment on a car when he was as broke as a joke. She was the one who tried to teach him to save money and to think beyond the hood. And when he had gotten hurt in a car accident, she took leave from her job to take care of him. Recalling all of her patience with him and sacrifices, Jaheim leaned down and kissed her on the cheek. The taste of her tears was a stark reminder that he had caused her to cry one too many times. He owed it to Aria to do right by her.

"I won't let him hurt you. I promise you that," he said.

"Please don't."

Jaheim walked into the kitchen area and returned with a knife. Carefully, he cut the duct tape from around Aria's arms, body and feet, freeing her from all restraints. "I want you to be happy even if it's not with me and I'm sorry that I couldn't be the man that you wanted me to be."

Aria stood up on unsteady legs and hugged him. "Thank you, Jah. In spite of everything, I wish you the best." Aria kissed him on the cheek.

"I appreciate that," he nodded. "Now, please get out of here before my nigga gets back and flips the script again."

Aria didn't have to be told to leave twice. She saw her phone laying on the table. She grabbed it and got ghost.

Chapter 25

Young Milli was going crazy with worry. He'd had one of his soldiers make the drop almost an hour ago but he had yet to hear back from the niggaz who'd snatched up Aria. The bread wasn't shit to him, he just wanted his girl back, safe and sound.

When the phone lit up with Aria's name flashing across the screen, he answered it in a reserved tone, expecting to receive another demand from the kidnapper. "Sup?"

"Bae, come and get me!" Aria cried.

Young Milli dropped the phone and looked toward Heaven. "Thank God." He wasn't religious but he believed in The Most High. Even for a shooter like himself. "Baby, do you know where you're at?"

Aria knew she was inside a Waffle House about a mile or so from the hotel. She was inside the ladies room, afraid to come come. "Excuse me. Can you tell me where this Waffle House is located?" she asked a lady who had just entered the restroom.

When the lady gave her the location, she relayed it to Young Milli.

"Don't move. And stay on the phone with me until I get there."

"My battery is low."

"Don't worry, I'mma do a hundred all the way to you."

***

"Unc, what the fuck do you mean you let her go?" Twan was heated.

"Just what I said." Jaheim had found his balls again. "Wasn't no reason to kill the girl. You wanted a hundred thousand dollars and you got it." He pointed to the stacks of money on the bed. "She's not going to the police on us and she don't know who you are, so you don't have to worry about her giving you up to her nigga and 'em."

"Maybe not, but we could've milked her nigga for some more bread. That nigga caked up, believe that. The way his people stomped us out, that was worth at least a quarter million. This shit is chump change."

Jaheim shook his head. A line from the movie Scarface came to mind. *See, the guy, he wants more than what he needs. He don't fly straight no more.*

"Youngsta, don't let greed be your God," cautioned Jaheim, sagely. Now that he had accepted that Aria deserved to live and be happy, he was thinking clearly. But Twan was on some other shit.

"Unc, miss me with that philosophy bullshit. You should'na let the bitch go. That was a weak ass move. You must still love that hoe."

"I do. But that's not the point." Jaheim thought of Aria's tears. He didn't regret letting her leave unharmed.

"What *is* your fuckin point?" Twan's voice boomed.

"She didn't deserve what you were gonna do to her. That ain't how I rock. I don't do dirt to anyone who hasn't done dirt to me. She deserved to move on with her life. I'm the one who fucked up not Aria."

Twan laughed, maniacally. "Nigga, you think this is about that fuck shit? I don't give a fuck about that punk ass shit! This is about those niggas putting hands and feet on us. And that bitch caused it all. I was gonna make her nigga pay us again, but you fucked it up!"

"We already got paid. Now you being greedy."

158

Twan's mouth turned down at the corners. He stepped chest to chest with Jaheim. Nose to nose. "Unc, I knew all along that you a sucka ass nigga. If that hoe send the police after you, I wouldn't put it pass you to flip on me."

"You think I'm a snitch?" Jaheim gritted.

"Ion know. I do know you're weak, though. And I could never trust a weak muthafucka." Twan took two steps backwards and whipped out his tool. "You let the bitch go. Now, I'ma give you what she was gon' get."

Jaheim lunged for the gun in Twan's hand.

Boom! Boom!

Twan watched the man he affectionately called Unc crash to the floor, face down. He put the gun to the back of Jaheim's head and finished him off, execution-style.

He hurriedly wiped down the room, then gathered up the money and got in the wind.

Ca$h & Destiny Skai

160

Chapter 26

Aria leaned against the bathroom stall nervously and held the phone to her ear. Every time the door opened, she jumped in fear that her captor would come looking for her. She checked the percentage of the phone and realized it wouldn't be long before it shut off completely.

"Bae, hurry please. My phone is about to shut off," she pleaded.

"I'm almost there. But if it does hang up, walk outside in twenty minutes," he promised. Milli drove like a Nascar driver to get to the woman that he had a genuine love for.

Within a matter of minutes, Aria's phone shut off in the middle of Milli talking. She watched the screen as it blacked out. "Shit!" she mumbled.

Aria stayed put for a while before exiting the restroom and going outside. Cautiously, she watched her surroundings as she stood next to the building and out of plain sight. Her head swiveled in the direction of every car that drove by. For a second, she could've sworn she saw Jaheim's car speed past the restaurant. That caused her heart to drop. However, all of that went away when she spotted Milli's car pulling into the parking lot. She waited until he came to a complete stop and got out of the car before she made her presence known.

Milli met Aria halfway as she bolted towards him and jumped into his arms. "I never thought I would see you again." She held him tightly.

"These last two days have been hell without you, and I wasn't going to rest until I got you back." Milli gently traced the dark ring underneath her eye. "Did you recognize the niggaz who did this to you?"

Aria told him that it was her ex and another guy whose face she never saw. "And I couldn't place his voice."

The bruise on her face had Young Milli ready to kill Jaheim and his sidekick. "This nigga gone pay for what he did to you."

"No." Aria placed her hand on his chest and looked into his eyes that had now formed into tiny slits. "You don't have to do that. His friend is the one that kidnapped me. Jaheim was the one that let me go."

Milli disagreed. He was adamant that it was Jaheim's fault in the first place. He vowed to do the most savage things to that muthafucka for what he had done to Aria. But when he saw how upset she became, he said, "A'ight. Since he let you go, I'ma give him a pass." But those words were only to appease Aria. There was no way Young Milli was letting that nigga walk away from this unscathed. *I'ma give it a little time, then I'm going to Florida and show him how an ATL nigga get down.*

"Bae, can we just get out of here, please?" Aria didn't want to spend another moment in that parking lot. "I'm ready to go home."

Milli opened the passenger door, so she could climb inside before getting into the driver's seat. "Where were they keeping you at?" he quizzed.

Aria pointed in the direction of the motel. "The Motel 6 up the street."

"Okay." Milli nodded his head and drove off contemplating his next move.

During the drive, Aria was quiet. She held onto Milli's right hand as he steered the wheel with the left one. Every so often he would glance at her while she took a cat nap. Just the thought of losing Aria made him realize that he loved her deeply in a short amount of time. No woman had ever had that effect on him, and he didn't want her to ever leave his side.

Back at the house, Aria felt completely safe once she was back under his watchful eye. Immediately, after their arrival she ran a hot bath and stripped out of the clothing and tossed them on the floor. Those items were going to the garbage. Aria didn't want a reminder of what happened the day after Christmas. The black eye was enough.

Aria stepped into the tub and lowered her body into the hot water and closed her eyes. It was relaxing until she felt someone touch her shoulder. She damn near jumped out of her skin, but quickly calmed herself when she saw Milli.

"Sorry, luv, I didn't mean to frighten you." Milli stroked the side of her cheek. "You're safe now and you have nothing else to worry about. I promise you that nothing like this will ever happen to you again."

"Okay," she nodded. Her trust in him was infinite.

"Are you hungry?" he asked.

"No. I just want to lay down." After sitting upright for days, in a hard ass chair, Aria wanted to rest on a comfortable mattress.

"A'ight. I'll be waiting on you."

"Can you get rid of my clothes? I'm never wearing that again."

"Yes." Milli picked up the items from the floor and left the bathroom.

Aria stayed in the tub until the water became lukewarm. Thirty minutes later, she was fully clean and dressed in her pajamas. As promised, Milli was sitting on the bed waiting on her. Aria climbed into the bed and snuggled underneath her protector. Milli held her in his arms until she fell asleep.

Later, Aria woke up long enough for Young Milli to massage her sore body, give her an ice pack for her eye. and bring her something light to eat. He waited until after Aria had eaten her food to tell her about Damu. She was saddened. "I know Amani is hurt," she said, remembering Damu's lovely lady who she had met at the Christmas dinner.

"She is. Thank goodness she has a strong support system." He knew that for sure. He also knew that the only thing that would truly help Amani's grief, short of bringing Damu back, was for him to get at BNK, who they all agreed was responsible for everything that transpired that night. Young Milli was definitely going to put something hot up in BNK.

Tearfully, Aria told him about her ordeal. Young Milli again promised her that from this day forward he would protect her with his last breath.

"What happened wasn't your fault, bae," she said. Then, she fell back to sleep, cuddled in his arms.

Chapter 27

It was December 30th, 2021, less than forty-eight hours before 2022 would announce itself in bold fashion across the nation. Last year at this time, the Covid-19 pandemic had kept most people indoors in Atlanta. A year ago, Young Milli and his crew had flown to Las Vegas on a private plane that he rented. Damu was there then, but he wouldn't be celebrating New Year with them this year, Young Milli reminisced. The other day, he had shipped Damu's body back to his family in Compton.

"I miss you, blood. If there's a heaven for a G, I know you and the other homies that have passed away are balling up there," Milli said as he pulled a black hoodie over his vest, tightened the hood around his chin, then checked his Draco. It was loaded with a 50-round *dick.*

A short while ago, Young Milli had seen BNK and one of his hittas on IG live. He recognized BNK's hitta as the nigga who had tried to kill him at Diamond's. Young Milli also recognized the sports bar they were at. He had to move fast before they left.

Aria woke up before he could creep out of the bedroom. "Bae, where are you sneaking off to?" she joked.

"I'll be back."

"That means you're going somewhere you don't want me to know," she guessed correctly.

"Exactly."

"But I don't want to be here alone."

"I'm sorry, luv. But I can't take you with me and I have to do this. You'll be safe here. Nobody who would be out to hurt you knows where I lay my head," he said from the doorway. "Besides, your ex let you go, so he's not a threat. And the other guy is probably somewhere living it up. He got the money, that's all he wanted."

"You're right, baby. Go handle your business. I love you."

"Huh?"

"Bae, you heard me. I said, *I love you.* You don't have to say it back." Aria wasn't going to keep it to herself anymore. She didn't care how unlikely her love for him was nor that it had happened in a short time.

During those two days that she was held hostage, she had been afraid she was going to die without ever telling him how she truly felt. She had known that she was in love with Young Milli two days after coming to Atlanta. She just hadn't wanted to sound silly or scare him off. So, she had held it in. But when Aria was facing death, she promised herself that if she ever saw Young Milli again she would tell him those three little words that were so huge in her heart.

"Save that until I get back," he said. He didn't want to be taken out of that killa zone he was in.

"Okay, be safe." She had no idea what Young Milli was about to do, but her words fit the situation perfectly.

Inside an old school car that had belonged to Damu, Young Milli pulled on his black leather gloves and made sure that he had his black ski mask. Then, he checked his Draco again for assurance. Satisfied that he was strapped and ready, he turned on the late Nipsey Hussle.

I ain't nothing like you fucking rap niggas
Hussle man a shooter, that's a fact, nigga
Thirty-two extendos in my mac, nigga

It was time to show BNK that their beef was bigger than rap.

166

Xmas in the Arms of an ATL Shooter

***

It was a little after 12 a.m. when Young Milli reached the parking lot of the establishment where he knew BNK was doing his IG live from, he checked the Gram to see if that nigga was still online stunting. Milli smiled when he saw the nigga sitting inside of his car, doing a whack ass freestyle rap for his followers.

I'm outchea in the city/ Litty like a bitch who's sadity/ Hard like the nipples of a titty/ The clip in my gun hold fiddy/ Kill a nigga and don't show no pity/ Baby mama thick and so pretty/Got my name tatted on her kitty

Young Milli drove around the lot until he spotted BNK's powder blue Phantom. He saw the flame of a lighter on the passenger side. That meant that BNK's hitta was still there, too. Young Milli parked close to the exit for a fast getaway. He pulled the ski mask down over his face and checked his semi-automatic for the third time. It was ready to spit lead.

BNK was still rapping online when a burst of bullets shattered the driver's window and ripped into his face. Young Milli snatched open the door and got up close and personal to his opps.

Boc! Boc! Boc! Boc! Boc! Boc!

BNK's face disintegrated. His hitta reached for the gun in his waist, but a second volley on gunfire opened up his head and chest. For good measure, Young Milli pumped another twenty shots in their bodies.

I told you I ain't nothing like you fucking rap niggas. Milli is a shooter, that's a fact nigga! Young Milli dashed back to the getaway car and sped off.

***

When Young Milli got home, Aria was sitting up in bed, watching *Love & Basketball.* He walked straight past her, headed to the bathroom. She got up out of bed to ask if he wanted her to run him a bath or go downstairs and get him a snack. That's when she saw blood all over his face and clothes.

"Bae, oh, my God! Are you hurt?" she cried.

"Nah, I'm good. Go back to bed."

"What happened?" She was looking him over, making sure he wasn't injured.

"The less you know, the better off we'll both be. But if anybody ever asks you where I was tonight, I was here with you and I never left the house. Now, go back to bed. I'll be in there soon."

"Okay, but can I ask you one question?"

"Yes, but I may not answer it," he said as he stripped off the rest of his clothes and dropped them in a plastic bag.

"Was it Jaheim?"

"No, luv. It wasn't. I put that on my mama."

Aria didn't need to hear anymore. If Milli swore on his mother, he was speaking the gospel truth.

After undressing, Young Milli took the bag of bloody clothes in the backyard and burned them. He bared the cold and showered in the yard with a water hose. If the police ever came to search his house for evidence of his involvement in the double murder of BNK and his homie, they wouldn't find traces of those nigga's blood inside Young Milli's shower. He had already gotten rid of the weapon and one of his soldiers was on the way to get the car he had driven. It would be taken to a remote location and set on fire.

"Damu, I handled that tonight. G's up, big homie," said Young Milli a few minutes later as he looked out of the large picture window in his living room and watched the old school Chevy being driven away. That had been one of Damu's prized possession, but he would definitely be pleased with what it had just been used for. *Much love, blood. RIP.* Young Milli touched his fist to his chest as the taillights of Damu's car faded into oblivion.

Now that he had dealt with his opps, it was time for Young Milli to get back to the business of loving on his Queen.

Chapter 28

Aria checked the weather for the third time that morning on Google. She and Milli were leaving for a quick getaway to bring in the New Year. New York City was their destination. Aria was hyped to see the ball drop. After everything they'd been through over the past few days it was truly needed. It was time to step away from the madness and regroup. Milli hadn't spoken another word about the incident since Aria saw him covered in blood, but she had her suspicions about what occurred.

Early that morning when Aria scrolled down her timeline on IG, she saw that BNK's murder was a trending topic. *I know bae killed his fat ass and he deserved that shit, too. All of this shit was his fault.* Aria knew not to ask any questions, so she pushed that subject to the back of her mind.

Aria tossed her phone into her purse and shoved a few extra items into her suitcase. In her mind, it was safer to over pack and have options. Besides, she had never been to New York and wanted to be prepared for the extremely cold weather.

Milli walked into the bedroom shaking his head with a smirk on his face and his hands in his pockets.

"What's so funny?"

"You." He sat down on the bed. "Why aren't you ready yet? It's time to go."

"I'm ready."

"Looks to me like you are still packing, ma'am," he chuckled.

"Oh, I'm ma'am now?" she hissed.

"Don't you call me *sir* sometimes?"

"My name is *luv* and don't you forget it," she sassed, then flashed a cue cute smile.

"Duly noted, luv. Let's go." Milli grabbed her suitcase, and they were on their way.

Aria stared out the window of the private jet, absorbing the breathtaking view from thirty thousand feet in the air. She looked over at Milli. "I don't think I ever want to ride on a commercial plane again. First class has nothing on this."
"You won't have to."
"Good because this is how I want to take all baecations."
"I got you."
On second thought, she asked "Did I sound boujee?"
"Not at all. Nothing but the best for my girl." He leaned over and kissed her face. The bruise under her eye had faded tremendously.

For the two hours they were up in the air, the loving couple listened to music and sipped on some champagne until they landed at the LaGuardia Airport. From there, a private car service drove them to the *Intercontinental New York* hotel. in the heart of Times Square. The suite was huge and immaculate. She couldn't wait to relax in the Jacuzzi tub. Aria stood in the window and peered over the city that was known to never sleep. Milli walked up behind her and wrapped his arms around her waist. She placed her hands on top of him and smiled.

They spent the early part of the day visiting a few well-known tourist spots. From there, they stopped and ate at Virgil's Real BBQ, a popular eatery Young Milli was familiar with, having been to New York numerous times. After the delicious early evening meal, Aria and Milli took the subway through the city. They posted up in front of the graffiti walls and snapped a few pics and put them on Instagram. They did the same in front of the Statue of Liberty.

Their next stop was the world-renowned Black Ink tattoo shop, famous for their dramatic reality show. Caesar, the owner jumped at the opportunity to tatt Young Milli since he was a fan of his music. Aria watched closely as the masterpiece came to life. Milli stood in front of the mirror to look at the finished product and was moved by the sentimental piece. It was a set of praying hands with beads and Damu's name, date of birth and death, encrypted on his skin.

"I love it," Aria screeched bringing her hand up to her mouth.

"Thanks, bae. It's your turn get up there."

Aria's tattoo took no more than an hour. She got an infinity symbol that read, *love conquers all*. The shop vibe was just like it was on television, but without the drama. They were drinking and dancing to Young Milli's music.

***

After leaving Black Ink, Young Milli and Aria went back to their suite where they chilled until it was 11:45 p.m., fifteen minutes away from bringing in 2022. Mixed in with the congested crowd, they wore designer masks and stayed close to one another, waiting for the ball to drop. Couples were dancing and singing as the song, *Start Spreading the News* played. Eventually, Aria and Milli joined in the fun with some light two-stepping. The temperature dropped, but the alcohol and their constant movement helped keep them warm.

Start spreading the news. I'm leaving today. I want to be a part of it. New York, New York. These vagabond shoes. They are longing to stray. Right through the very heart of it. New York, New York.

Bright lights lit up the city and the stars lit up the sky. People from all walks of life were in attendance to celebrate a new beginning with their significant others. It felt good to be amongst a crowd of friendly folks, no opps for Milli to beef with and no one looking to cause Aria harm. Everyone had their phones out, recording and snapping pictures. Young Milli felt like he was at one of his concerts.

On one of the buildings, they could see where the countdown began starting with the number twenty. On another billboard, 2022, flashed repeatedly, along with the words Happy New Year. The crowd called every number out in sync with one another. Five, four, three, two, one—Happy New Year, everyone shouted. Confetti fell onto the crowd and fireworks lit up the sky. It was a magical moment for the both of them. Young Milli reached in his pocket for the surprise he had for Aria, but he had left it in the suite. *Damn!* He was disappointed in himself; he had blown the moment, but he played it off.

Milli turned to face Aria. "Happy New Year, luv." Then he planted a passionate kiss to her soft lips and hugged her tightly in his arms. "What is your New Year's resolution?"

"To live life every day like it's my last and without regret."

"I second that." Milli kissed her hand. "My resolution is to introduce you to something new every month."

"I like the sound of that." Aria smiled.

As they made their way back to the room, Milli stopped in front of a rugged, homeless black man shaking a cup and asking for food. Milli stopped in his tracks and pulled out a wad of cash. He peeled off a stack of bills and placed them in the man's cup. "Happy New Year, old school. Stay warm."

"Thank you. Thank you, good brother. God bless you."

"God bless you, too."

Aria waited until they walked away to say something. "Why did you give him so much money?"

"Sometimes a man has to do a few good deeds to balance out his sins."

"You are so thoughtful and generous." Aria leaned her head on his shoulder, as they continued their journey.

Chapter 29

The following morning, Aria and Milli sat in the Jacuzzi tub sipping on some Casamigos for breakfast and listening to Pop Smoke's *Yeah, Yeah* remix with Queen Naija. When her part came up Aria sang loudly for Milli, while straddling his lap with her finger on his lip.

"You know I love that thug shit. Know I love that rough shit. You know I'm a good girl, but I just might let you touch it. And you can't seem to stay up out of trouble, but I love it. If I'm your ride or die, baby, I want all or nothing. Understand when the streets be callin' your name. I'll be waitin' up for you, it's all part of the game. I know what I signed up for when I tattooed your name on my heart, still holding you down, like I been from the start."

Once Queen Naija's part was over, she laughed. "You like that don't you?"

"Hell yeah!" She had Milli hyped. "Come on, luv, you gotta get in the studio with me and do a duet. Not no Ike and Tina shit, though," he laughed.

"You know how I feel about that."

"Damn, I thought you loved a nigga." He turned his head to the side like he was mad, but he really wasn't.

"Okay, big baby. I'll think about it. But I'm not making any promises." She pecked his lips.

Milli's phone rang. He looked down at the screen and saw that it was his attorney's name pop up. "Bae, turn the music off for a second. I gotta take this call. It's my lawyer. It has to be urgent, or he would've messaged me." He waited until it was quiet to pick up. "Hello."

"Young Milli, my friend. Happy New Year!"

"Same to you." Young Milli waited for him to drop a bomb.

"I know you're probably on vacation, but I had to call you. A detective with the Atlanta Police Department called me not too long ago. They want you to come in for questioning about the December 30th murder of a rapper known as BNK. They're curious about your whereabouts on the night in question. From what I gather, they suspect that his death has a connection to the alleged events that took place at a different nightclub a few days prior."

"I was at home with my girl the entire night of December 30th. I didn't leave out of the house at all." Aria's eyes locked in with Milli's.

"Okay. When you get back come and see me and we'll go down so you can make a statement. Otherwise, they'll issue a warrant for your arrest."

"I'll call you when I touch down."

"That's fine. Make sure that your alibi witness is solid. I'm sure they'll want to question her."

"No problem. My alibi is airtight." Milli hung up and sat the phone back on the side of the tub. He looked up at Aria. "How hard do you fuck with me?"

"Hard as fuck," she promised.

"Can I count on that?"

"Didn't your mother tell you that I am the one?" She took his face in her hands and looked him the eye. "I got you, baby. Just give me the game plan." She intuitively knew what this was about. *The night he came home with blood all over him.*

"They're gonna threaten you. Try to scare you. Tell you that I'm a thug and you shouldn't lie to protect me. Yada, yada, yada. All I need you to do is stick to the script. Can you do that under pressure?"

"Bae, that's not pressure. Pressure is the thought of what we have coming to an end. I will protect that with my all," she swore.

178

"If they were to take me to trial, they'll force you to take the witness stand. The judge will threaten you with prison time if you lie under oath." Young Milli paused to gather his thoughts. He wasn't trying to have Aria risk her freedom."

"Bae, they can threaten me with life. I still wouldn't testify against you. I'm not claiming to be a gangsta chick. But I am your ride or die. When I love, I love hard. I'm not flipping on my man," she maintained. "You've been too good to me for me to do you like that."

Young Milli believed her. But another thought came to mind. One that would protect her from ever having to testify against him. He took her hands and held them in his. "I appreciate your loyalty, Aria. Real talk. Because most of these niggas in the streets who are supposed to be killas and gangstas fold under pressure. But I have a solution to this problem. One that I hope will make us both happy for years to come."

Aria had no idea what Young Milli's solution would be. "Bae, tell me what it is."

"They can't force a man's wife to testify against him. That's law. It's called spousal privilege. I read about it a few years ago," he explained.

Aria saw in his face that he was serious. "Are you really asking me to marry you?"

"Yes, luv," he said.

"Milli, I would love to be your wife. But not like this. You don't have to marry me to assure my loyalty. I told you I got you, and I do."

Milli shook his head and chuckled. "So, you think that's the only reason a nigga asking you to marry me?"

"It is, isn't it?" She lowered her head and eyes.

"Shorty, you got jokes."

Young Milli hopped out of the Jacuzzi and went into the bedroom. When he came back, he extended a hand to Aria and helped her out of the water. She saw a smirk on his face.

"Milli, what are you up to?"

He brought his other hand from behind his back. In his palm was a beautiful ten-carat diamond wedding ring.

"*Bam!*" Milli held it up for her to admire. "Asking you to marry me was my plan all along. I would've done it at midnight last night, but I left the ring in the room," he smiled.

"Milli, oh bae, this can't be happening." Happy tears streaked down Aria's face.

Young Milli's smile widened as he went down on one knee.

THE END

Lock Down Publications and Ca$h Presents assisted publishing packages.

BASIC PACKAGE $499
Editing
Cover Design
Formatting

UPGRADED PACKAGE $800
Typing
Editing
Cover Design
Formatting

ADVANCE PACKAGE $1,200
Typing
Editing
Cover Design
Formatting
Copyright registration
Proofreading
Upload book to Amazon

LDP SUPREME PACKAGE $1,500
Typing
Editing
Cover Design
Formatting
Copyright registration
Proofreading
Set up Amazon account

Upload book to Amazon
Advertise on LDP Amazon and Facebook page

***Other services available upon request. Additional
charges may apply
Lock Down Publications
P.O. Box 944
Stockbridge, GA 30281-9998
Phone # 470 303-9761

Submission Guideline

Submit the first three chapters of your completed manuscript to ldpsubmissions@gmail.com, subject line: Your book's title. The manuscript must be in a .doc file and sent as an attachment. Document should be in Times New Roman, double spaced and in size 12 font. Also, provide your synopsis and full contact information. If sending multiple submissions, they must each be in a separate email.

Have a story but no way to send it electronically? You can still submit to LDP/Ca$h Presents. Send in the first three chapters, written or typed, of your completed manuscript to:

LDP: Submissions Dept
Po Box 944
Stockbridge, Ga 30281

DO NOT send original manuscript. Must be a duplicate.

Provide your synopsis and a cover letter containing your full contact information.

Thanks for considering LDP and Ca$h Presents.

NEW RELEASES

CONFESSIONS OF A JACKBOY II by NICHOLAS
LOCK
A GANGSTA'S KARMA 2 by FLAME
GRIMEY WAYS by RAY VINCI
A GANGSTA SAVED XMAS by MONET DRAGUN
XMAS WITH AN ATL SHOOTER by CA$H & DES-
TINY SKAI

Coming Soon from Lock Down Publications/Ca$h Presents

BLOOD OF A BOSS **VI**

SHADOWS OF THE GAME II

TRAP BASTARD II

By **Askari**

LOYAL TO THE GAME **IV**

By **T.J. & Jelissa**

IF TRUE SAVAGE **VIII**

MIDNIGHT CARTEL IV

DOPE BOY MAGIC IV

CITY OF KINGZ III

NIGHTMARE ON SILENT AVE II

By **Chris Green**

BLAST FOR ME **III**

A SAVAGE DOPEBOY III

CUTTHROAT MAFIA III

DUFFLE BAG CARTEL VII

HEARTLESS GOON VI

By **Ghost**

A HUSTLER'S DECEIT III

KILL ZONE II

BAE BELONGS TO ME III

By **Aryanna**

KING OF THE TRAP III

By **T.J. Edwards**

GORILLAZ IN THE BAY V

3X KRAZY III

STRAIGHT BEAST MODE II

De'Kari

KINGPIN KILLAZ IV

STREET KINGS III

PAID IN BLOOD III

CARTEL KILLAZ IV

DOPE GODS III

Hood Rich

SINS OF A HUSTLA II

ASAD

RICH $AVAGE II

MONEY IN THE GRAVE II

By Martell Troublesome Bolden

YAYO V

Bred In The Game 2

S. Allen

CREAM III

By Yolanda Moore

SON OF A DOPE FIEND III

HEAVEN GOT A GHETTO II

By Renta

LOYALTY AIN'T PROMISED III

By Keith Williams

I'M NOTHING WITHOUT HIS LOVE II

SINS OF A THUG II

TO THE THUG I LOVED BEFORE II

By Monet Dragun

QUIET MONEY IV

EXTENDED CLIP III

THUG LIFE IV

By **Trai'Quan**

THE STREETS MADE ME IV

By **Larry D. Wright**

IF YOU CROSS ME ONCE II

By **Anthony Fields**

THE STREETS WILL NEVER CLOSE II

By **K'ajji**

HARD AND RUTHLESS III

THE BILLIONAIRE BENTLEYS II

Von Diesel

KILLA KOUNTY II

By Khufu

MONEY GAME III

By Smoove Dolla

JACK BOYZ VERSUS DOPE BOYZ

By Romell Tukes

MURDA WAS THE CASE II

Elijah R. Freeman

THE STREETS NEVER LET GO II

By Robert Baptiste

AN UNFORESEEN LOVE III

By **Meesha**

KING OF THE TRENCHES II

by **GHOST & TRANAY ADAMS**

MONEY MAFIA II

LOYAL TO THE SOIL II

By **Jibril Williams**

QUEEN OF THE ZOO II

By **Black Migo**

THE BRICK MAN III

By King Rio

VICIOUS LOYALTY II

By Kingpen

A GANGSTA'S PAIN II

By J-Blunt

CONFESSIONS OF A JACKBOY III

By Nicholas Lock

GRIMEY WAYS II

By Ray Vinci

Available Now

RESTRAINING ORDER **I & II**

By **CA$H & Coffee**

LOVE KNOWS NO BOUNDARIES **I II & III**

By **Coffee**

RAISED AS A GOON I, II, III & IV

BRED BY THE SLUMS I, II, III

BLAST FOR ME I & II

ROTTEN TO THE CORE I II III

A BRONX TALE I, II, III

DUFFLE BAG CARTEL I II III IV V VI

HEARTLESS GOON I II III IV V

A SAVAGE DOPEBOY I II

DRUG LORDS I II III

CUTTHROAT MAFIA I II

KING OF THE TRENCHES

By **Ghost**

LAY IT DOWN **I & II**

LAST OF A DYING BREED I II

BLOOD STAINS OF A SHOTTA I & II III

By **Jamaica**

LOYAL TO THE GAME I II III

LIFE OF SIN I, II III

By **TJ & Jelissa**

BLOODY COMMAS I & II

SKI MASK CARTEL I II & III

KING OF NEW YORK I II,III IV V

RISE TO POWER I II III

COKE KINGS I II III IV V

BORN HEARTLESS I II III IV

KING OF THE TRAP I II

By **T.J. Edwards**

IF LOVING HIM IS WRONG…I & II

LOVE ME EVEN WHEN IT HURTS I II III

By **Jelissa**

WHEN THE STREETS CLAP BACK I & II III

THE HEART OF A SAVAGE I II III

MONEY MAFIA

LOYAL TO THE SOIL

By **Jibril Williams**

A DISTINGUISHED THUG STOLE MY HEART I II & III

LOVE SHOULDN'T HURT I II III IV

RENEGADE BOYS I II III IV

PAID IN KARMA I II III

SAVAGE STORMS I II

AN UNFORESEEN LOVE I II

By **Meesha**

A GANGSTER'S CODE I &, II III

A GANGSTER'S SYN I II III

THE SAVAGE LIFE I II III

CHAINED TO THE STREETS I II III

BLOOD ON THE MONEY I II III

A GANGSTA'S PAIN

By **J-Blunt**

PUSH IT TO THE LIMIT

By **Bre' Hayes**

BLOOD OF A BOSS **I, II, III, IV, V**

SHADOWS OF THE GAME

TRAP BASTARD

By **Askari**

THE STREETS BLEED MURDER **I, II & III**

THE HEART OF A GANGSTA I II& III

Xmas in the Arms of an ATL Shooter

By **Jerry Jackson**

CUM FOR ME I II III IV V VI VII

An **LDP Erotica Collaboration**

BRIDE OF A HUSTLA **I II & II**

THE FETTI GIRLS **I, II& III**

CORRUPTED BY A GANGSTA I, II III, IV

BLINDED BY HIS LOVE

THE PRICE YOU PAY FOR LOVE I, II ,III

DOPE GIRL MAGIC I II III

By **Destiny Skai**

WHEN A GOOD GIRL GOES BAD

By **Adrienne**

THE COST OF LOYALTY I II III

By Kweli

A GANGSTER'S REVENGE **I II III & IV**

THE BOSS MAN'S DAUGHTERS I II III IV V

A SAVAGE LOVE **I & II**

BAE BELONGS TO ME I II

A HUSTLER'S DECEIT I, II, III

WHAT BAD BITCHES DO I, II, III

SOUL OF A MONSTER I II III

KILL ZONE

A DOPE BOY'S QUEEN I II III

By **Aryanna**

A KINGPIN'S AMBITON

A KINGPIN'S AMBITION **II**

I MURDER FOR THE DOUGH

By **Ambitious**

TRUE SAVAGE I II III IV V VI VII

DOPE BOY MAGIC I, II, III

MIDNIGHT CARTEL I II III

CITY OF KINGZ I II

NIGHTMARE ON SILENT AVE

By **Chris Green**

A DOPEBOY'S PRAYER

By **Eddie "Wolf" Lee**

THE KING CARTEL **I, II & III**

By **Frank Gresham**

THESE NIGGAS AIN'T LOYAL **I, II & III**

By **Nikki Tee**

GANGSTA SHYT **I II &III**

By **CATO**

THE ULTIMATE BETRAYAL

By **Phoenix**

BOSS'N UP **I , II & III**

By **Royal Nicole**

I LOVE YOU TO DEATH

By **Destiny J**

I RIDE FOR MY HITTA

I STILL RIDE FOR MY HITTA

By **Misty Holt**

LOVE & CHASIN' PAPER

By **Qay Crockett**

TO DIE IN VAIN

Xmas in the Arms of an ATL Shooter

SINS OF A HUSTLA

By **ASAD**

BROOKLYN HUSTLAZ

By **Boogsy Morina**

BROOKLYN ON LOCK I & II

By **Sonovia**

GANGSTA CITY

By **Teddy Duke**

A DRUG KING AND HIS DIAMOND I & II III

A DOPEMAN'S RICHES

HER MAN, MINE'S TOO I, II

CASH MONEY HO'S

THE WIFEY I USED TO BE I II

By Nicole Goosby

TRAPHOUSE KING **I II & III**

KINGPIN KILLAZ I II III

STREET KINGS I II

PAID IN BLOOD **I II**

CARTEL KILLAZ I II III

DOPE GODS I II

By **Hood Rich**

LIPSTICK KILLAH **I, II, III**

CRIME OF PASSION I II & III

FRIEND OR FOE I II III

By **Mimi**

STEADY MOBBN' **I, II, III**

THE STREETS STAINED MY SOUL I II

By **Marcellus Allen**
WHO SHOT YA **I, II, III**
SON OF A DOPE FIEND I II
HEAVEN GOT A GHETTO
Renta
GORILLAZ IN THE BAY **I II III IV**
TEARS OF A GANGSTA I II
3X KRAZY I II
STRAIGHT BEAST MODE
DE'KARI
TRIGGADALE I II III
MURDAROBER WAS THE CASE
Elijah R. Freeman
GOD BLESS THE TRAPPERS I, II, III
THESE SCANDALOUS STREETS I, II, III
FEAR MY GANGSTA I, II, III IV, V
THESE STREETS DON'T LOVE NOBODY I, II
BURY ME A G I, II, III, IV, V
A GANGSTA'S EMPIRE I, II, III, IV
THE DOPEMAN'S BODYGAURD I II
THE REALEST KILLAZ I II III
THE LAST OF THE OGS I II III
Tranay Adams
THE STREETS ARE CALLING
Duquie Wilson
MARRIED TO A BOSS I II III
By Destiny Skai & Chris Green

Xmas in the Arms of an ATL Shooter

KINGZ OF THE GAME I II III IV V VI

Playa Ray

SLAUGHTER GANG I II III

RUTHLESS HEART I II III

By Willie Slaughter

FUK SHYT

By Blakk Diamond

DON'T F#CK WITH MY HEART I II

By Linnea

ADDICTED TO THE DRAMA I II III

IN THE ARM OF HIS BOSS II

By Jamila

YAYO I II III IV

A SHOOTER'S AMBITION I II

BRED IN THE GAME

By S. Allen

TRAP GOD I II III

RICH $AVAGE

MONEY IN THE GRAVE I II

By Martell Troublesome Bolden

FOREVER GANGSTA

GLOCKS ON SATIN SHEETS I II

By Adrian Dulan

TOE TAGZ I II III

LEVELS TO THIS SHYT I II

By Ah'Million

KINGPIN DREAMS I II III

By Paper Boi Rari

CONFESSIONS OF A GANGSTA I II III IV

CONFESSIONS OF A JACKBOY I II

By Nicholas Lock

I'M NOTHING WITHOUT HIS LOVE

SINS OF A THUG

TO THE THUG I LOVED BEFORE

A GANGSTA SAVED XMAS

By Monet Dragun

CAUGHT UP IN THE LIFE I II III

THE STREETS NEVER LET GO

By Robert Baptiste

NEW TO THE GAME I II III

MONEY, MURDER & MEMORIES I II III

By **Malik D. Rice**

LIFE OF A SAVAGE I II III

A GANGSTA'S QUR'AN I II III

MURDA SEASON I II III

GANGLAND CARTEL I II III

CHI'RAQ GANGSTAS I II III

KILLERS ON ELM STREET I II III

JACK BOYZ N DA BRONX I II III

A DOPEBOY'S DREAM I II III

By **Romell Tukes**

LOYALTY AIN'T PROMISED I II

By Keith Williams

QUIET MONEY I II III

Xmas in the Arms of an ATL Shooter

THUG LIFE I II III

EXTENDED CLIP I II

By **Trai'Quan**

THE STREETS MADE ME I II III

By **Larry D. Wright**

THE ULTIMATE SACRIFICE I, II, III, IV, V, VI

KHADIFI

IF YOU CROSS ME ONCE

ANGEL I II

IN THE BLINK OF AN EYE

By **Anthony Fields**

THE LIFE OF A HOOD STAR

By **Ca$h & Rashia Wilson**

THE STREETS WILL NEVER CLOSE

By **K'ajji**

CREAM I II

By **Yolanda Moore**

NIGHTMARES OF A HUSTLA I II III

By **King Dream**

CONCRETE KILLA I II

VICIOUS LOYALTY

By **Kingpen**

HARD AND RUTHLESS I II

MOB TOWN 251

THE BILLIONAIRE BENTLEYS

By **Von Diesel**

GHOST MOB

Stilloan Robinson

MOB TIES I II III IV

By SayNoMore

BODYMORE MURDERLAND I II III

By Delmont Player

FOR THE LOVE OF A BOSS

By C. D. Blue

MOBBED UP I II III IV

THE BRICK MAN I II

By King Rio

KILLA KOUNTY

By Khufu

MONEY GAME I II

By Smoove Dolla

A GANGSTA'S KARMA I II

By FLAME

KING OF THE TRENCHES II

by **GHOST & TRANAY ADAMS**

QUEEN OF THE ZOO

By **Black Migo**

GRIMEY WAYS

By Ray Vinci

XMAS WITH AN ATL SHOOTER

By Ca$h & Destiny Skai

BOOKS BY LDP'S CEO, CA$H

TRUST IN NO MAN

TRUST IN NO MAN 2

TRUST IN NO MAN 3

BONDED BY BLOOD

SHORTY GOT A THUG

THUGS CRY

THUGS CRY 2

THUGS CRY 3

TRUST NO BITCH

TRUST NO BITCH 2

TRUST NO BITCH 3

TIL MY CASKET DROPS

RESTRAINING ORDER

RESTRAINING ORDER 2

IN LOVE WITH A CONVICT

LIFE OF A HOOD STAR

XMAS WITH AN ATL SHOOTER

www.ingramcontent.com/pod-product-compliance
Lightning Source LLC
Chambersburg PA
CBHW070507260626
47161CB00004B/1484